the rundown

the rundown

A Novel by Dean Wesley Smith
Based on the motion picture screenplay written by
R.J. Stewart and James Vanderbilt

POCKET STAR BOOKS
New York   London   Toronto   Sydney   Singapore

This book is a work of fiction. Names, characters, places and incidents are products of the author's imagination or are used fictitiously. Any resemblance to actual events or locales or persons living or dead is entirely coincidental.

An *Original* Publication of POCKET BOOKS

A Pocket Star Book published by
POCKET BOOKS, a division of Simon & Schuster, Inc.
1230 Avenue of the Americas, New York, NY 10020

ISBN: 0-7434-8094-5

First Pocket Books printing September 2003

10 9 8 7 6 5 4 3 2 1

POCKET STAR BOOKS and colophon are registered trademarks of Simon & Schuster, Inc.

Manufactured in the United States of America

For information regarding special discounts for bulk purchases, please contact Simon & Schuster Special Sales at 1-800-456-6798 or business@simonandschuster.com.

For John O.

Thanks

the rundown

ONE

Beck turned his pickup truck onto the long, palm-lined boulevard. Expensive cars lined the curbs for blocks, signaling to anyone driving on the four-lane Los Angeles street that there was something nearby that was important to the rich and trendy. In this case, it was a nightclub, the place to be this week for the in-crowd of Hollywood and the rest of the Southern California area.

Next week, Beck was sure, it would be a different club, on a different street. It always was. For him, the names of the clubs blended together into a blur, and he hadn't bothered to learn the name of this place any more than the others.

Couples and small groups of people stood along the sidewalk, sometimes leaning against their cars, as if being close to the club was enough. More than likely none of them had the clout, or the money, to get in. To Beck, there was nothing more pathetic than a wanna-be trendy.

The high palm trees and the orange street-lights gave the entire area along the boulevard the feeling of being on a stage, and the low night haze and smog blocked out any chance of seeing the night sky, creating even more of a closed-in feeling.

Hundreds of life dramas played out on this street, in this club, and along the sidewalks. Tonight Beck was going to be a player in one of those acts, even though the main actor named Knappmiller didn't yet know Beck was even coming. And more than likely Knappmiller wasn't going to like having the starring role.

The area around the front door of the club looked a lot like a mob scene jammed into the middle of a stage. This wasn't a normal mob with its high-fashion clothes and trendy looks. This mob didn't rebel against any police, only the guards at the doors as the flashes of paparazzi cameras cut the night air like faint bursts of lightning, freezing moments in time in bright, white light.

Beck knew the club well, including the layout, the main man at the door, and the owner. It wasn't a place he would ever go on his own time, but tonight wasn't his own time. Tonight he had a job to do.

Beck's older-model pickup looked clearly out of place driving past the rows of Porsches, Jags, and Mercedes. And he had counted on that. No one in this crowd would even dare to give him a second look as he went by, his driver's window open, letting in the thick evening air.

On the pickup's radio, Beck had been listening to a cooking show as he worked his way across town, and he half-wanted to stop and park and wait on the job until the show was over, but he knew that wasn't a good idea. Not now, not this close to the club, and not with Rudy waiting.

"Welcome back to Food Radio," the radio host said as the ad for an impotency drug ended. "We're talking with Chef Gilberto Oso about his famous ricotta ravioli."

Beck snorted. He could make better ravioli

than Gilberto, but somehow this guy had made a name for himself. Beck had tried the man's ravioli twice and couldn't put his finger on the trick to his recipe. It clearly had a strange aftertaste to it that Beck wasn't sure he liked.

As the chef rambled on, Beck quickly scanned the crowd at the club entrance as he drove past, seeing no one that worried him. Rudy, one of the waiters in the club, had called him when Knappmiller showed up, and Beck knew he didn't even need to hurry to get there. Knappmiller was known for his late-night partying. The target of this job wasn't going anywhere.

Beck swung the pickup down a side street and then into an alley that lead to the area behind the club. He paid close attention to the garbage cans and closed doors of buildings with one part of his mind while listening to the radio with the other. The sour smell of rotted food and spoiled booze cut through the cab, but Beck ignored it.

"A good recipe," the chef said, "you know, comes down to something, shall we say, unexpected."

Ahead in the alley Beck could see the scrawny shape of Rudy step forward from the club's service entrance. He was dressed in his black waiter's

4

uniform, and he clutched a half-smoked cigarette between his fingers. Rudy got paid by the same people that paid Beck, and never once had Beck not seen the kid look nervous. Right now, even in the dim alley light, Rudy looked like he might shake apart.

"For me," the chef said, his phony Italian accent filling the cab of the pickup, "it was just a sprinkle of nutmeg. Like-a magic dust-a."

Beck shook his head and pulled the truck into a spot across from the club's back door and out of the way. No wonder Beck liked his own ravioli better than this phony clown of a chef.

"Basil, pine nuts, and nutmeg," the chef said before Beck could switch off the radio in disgust. Pine nuts and nutmeg in ravioli? What would they come up with next?

As Beck cut the engine, Rudy stuck his head in the open window. "Knappmiller's on his third round."

Beck rolled up the window and pushed the door open, forcing Rudy to step back. "What's he drinking?"

"Jägermeisters and tequila," Rudy said while looking nervously up and down the alley.

Beck shook his head. One nasty combination

of drinks. He straightened his tailor-made suit, and brushed a wrinkle out of the silk. Then he faced the nervous waiter. "Any security?"

"No," Rudy said, turning and heading for the back door of the club, "but there's a slight problem."

Beck didn't ask. At this point it was just better to check out the problem for himself.

Rudy held the door open for Beck, then led him through the back area between the cartons of empty liquor bottles and the service storage areas. They then pushed through a heavy fire door, and went down a hallway to the club's VIP room.

The music in the club was loud, but not enough to block decent talking, and even though the no-smoking ban for bars and restaurants had been in place in California for a while, the VIP room seemed to have a smoke haze to it. The top of this particular food chain seemed to think that no law actually applied to them, and were always startled when one did.

A dozen tables, all linen-covered and large, filled the room, with a one-way glass wall between the room and the main part of the club so that people in the VIP room could feel superior to the poor souls who could only get into the main area.

And those in the main area felt that they were above the hopefuls on the sidewalk outside.

A food chain that actually had no meaning in any real world outside the made-up one these people lived in. And very soon one of these people named Knappmiller was going to discover there was a different food chain that he didn't rank on.

Beck studied the crowd in the main area through the one-way window, scanning for any trouble. Beck had no doubt that all those people on the other side of that glass hated looking at their own images, knowing the truly favored were behind the big mirror.

Nothing caught Beck's attention in the large crowd, so he turned his focus back to the task at hand. Knappmiller, his target, sat at a table on the far side of the VIP room.

Beck could see the problem that Rudy mentioned Brian Knappmiller, star quarterback for the Miami Dolphins, was surrounded by four of his teammates and a half dozen large-breasted women, more than likely expensive call girls.

"Guy on the left is Jalil Johnson," Rudy said. "I think he's left tackle or something."

Beck glanced at the small waiter standing beside him. "*Jamil* Johnson, six-time All Pro and future Hall of Famer."

Rudy just shrugged. "Jamil, Jalil, Jalopy, whatever."

Beck shook his head. "The guy next to him is Kambui Womble. He ran for two thousand yards last year and beat the toughest D in the league."

"Not to mention a murder charge," Rudy said. "Ice pick in the face, right?"

Beck ignored the comment and went on. "The other two guys are Jimmy Coggeshall and Davey Mulaire, first-round picks from USC and Ohio State, respectively."

Rudy just shrugged. "And last but not least, Brian Knappmiller. Throws like Joe Namath, bets like Pete Rose. Ladies and gentlemen, the Super Bowl Champions."

Rudy made a motion that made it clear that he didn't care at all what they had done. Then he turned and headed toward the bar to go back to work.

Beck cared. He had watched the game they won, and had been impressed. But he didn't dare let that show too much. He had a job to do.

He took a deep breath and started across the

room around the tables, taking careful inventory of the details along the way.

He spotted the second exit door.

He noted the empty table next to the players, with two big, empty chairs pushed into it.

He studied for a few steps the big gold cross and heavy chain around Jamil's neck.

And made special note of the bulge beneath Knappmiller's jacket. More than likely Jamil was armed as well, but Beck doubted the two rookies were. Too green, too fresh in town to be carrying.

Beck stopped in front of Knappmiller and took a moment to just stare at one of the best quarterbacks to ever play the game. Then keeping his voice level and polite, he said, "Excuse me, sorry to bother you, but—"

Knappmiller glanced up, clearly annoyed and studied Beck for a long moment. Then he said, "I got no pull at tryouts, man. Just show up at camp like everyone else."

Beck smiled at the assumption. It was good that Knappmiller sized him up to be someone who was big enough to play professional football.

"Actually, that's not what I—"

"Oh, I get it," Knappmiller said, now clearly annoyed.

He grabbed a pen from the inside of his jacket, slid a drink napkin over and looked up. "Who do I make it for?"

"Well, Beck would be fine."

Knappmiller slashed out the autograph and handed it up to Beck. "Best wishes, pal."

Beck studied the autograph for a moment. He was very pleased that he had it. It would make a nice addition to his collection. He hadn't expected to get it, considering what he was here to do.

He folded the napkin carefully, and put it in his pocket, then he turned and pulled up an empty chair, sliding it close to Knappmiller.

"Hey, what the—"

"A few months ago," Beck said, not giving the quarterback a chance to say anything more, "you made some wagers with an associate of mine."

Beck noticed that most of the talking around the table suddenly stopped, leaving only the music and the background noise from the other tables.

Knappmiller seemed actually shaken for a moment.

"Yo, whassup, Knappy?" Jamil asked, glaring at Beck.

Beck kept his gaze level and focused on Knappmiller.

"Nothin', nothin'."

"Actually," Beck said, "it was fifty thousand dollars that seems to be a little past due."

Beck watched as Knappmiller stared at him, trying to get Beck to back down. A lot rougher and stronger men had tried the same trick. Some of them were still not feeling well.

Around them the table was totally silent.

The call girls seemed to fade back and shift out of the way, letting the big football players deal with the intruder. Clearly they were real pros who could spot trouble when they saw it, and to them Beck was trouble.

Suddenly Knappmiller started to laugh, at first forced, then sounding more natural. He broke the stare with Beck and dug out a fat roll of cash, peeling off a large part of it.

"Okay, I got you, dude," Knappmiller said, counting as he went. "You're just a hardworking schmuck trying to do the right thing. I understand."

Beck didn't allow himself to move or even nod. It wasn't that he was doing the right thing; the key was if Knappmiller was going to do the right thing or not.

"Here's five grand to get you started."

Knappmiller shoved the money at Beck.

It was clear from the size of the roll of cash left that Knappmiller didn't have anywhere near the fifty thousand on him, and from what Billy had said, the quarterback was short in his accounts as well.

Beck took the money and stashed it in his inside jacket pocket. "The thing is, I've been told to get some collateral from you as well for the rest."

Knappmiller actually seemed puzzled for a moment, as if he didn't really know the meaning of the word.

"Collateral?"

Beck lowered his gaze until he was staring at the Super Bowl ring on Knappmiller's finger. It was a big one, looking out of proportion even on the quarterback's large hand. The ring was a combination of silver, gold, and diamonds, with the Super Bowl number and logo on it. Beck always thought the Super Bowl rings were the perfect combination of gaudy and beautiful.

And Knappmiller had earned that one.

It took a moment for Knappmiller to realize what Beck meant by the look. But when he did, Beck could sense an anger come up over the quarterback that wasn't going to be easy to contain. He had fought hard for that ring, and no one was going to take it easily.

"Get the hell outta here," Knappmiller said, his voice low and cold.

"Just give me the ring and you can go on with your party," Beck said. "No harm, no foul, as it were."

Before Beck could even duck aside, Jamil flipped a glass of Jäger into his face. The liqueur was room temperature and the smell almost made Beck gag since some of it went up his nose.

Beck stood his ground, but it took every bit of his self-control to not tear Jamil apart. He first would have to clean up, then he would finish this job.

"Maybe you didn't hear the man?" Jamil said.

Rudy suddenly appeared at Beck's side, but Beck held up a hand for the nervous waiter to stop. He took a handkerchief out of his breast pocket and patted the liquid from his face, then he slowly stood.

All of the football players stood with him as the partyers in the entire VIP room went silent, watching.

"What?" Coggeshall demanded, staring at Beck. "You wanna jump? C'mon, bitch!"

Beck shook his head and turned his back on the men. He needed to clean up and calm down before he took these men on, or he would hurt one of them, and damage their careers, and that wasn't what he was here to do. It wasn't their fault that their quarterback didn't have the sense to pay his gambling bills.

Rudy moved away from the table with him as the football players laughed and threw breadsticks.

"That's right, keep walking, big boy," Knappmiller shouted, then laughed.

Beck ignored him. He was only walking away to get his control back. Those idiots didn't know it, but he was doing them a favor.

Rudy scampered ahead of Beck out of the room and down the hall to the men's room, quickly checking to make sure they were alone.

Beck pulled out his cell phone and his boss's number, then with the phone against his ear, he wet a paper towel and dabbed at the brown liqueur that had soaked into his jacket.

"Leave it alone," Rudy said. "You'll set the stain."

"It's just prune juice," Beck said.

"What?" Rudy said, giving him a look as the phone rang on the other end.

"Didn't you know Jäger was—"

"Yeah!" Billy's deep, rough voice answered the phone.

"It's me," Beck said. "There's a little problem bringing it out. They're being somewhat truculent."

"They?" Billy asked.

"Yeah, they," Beck said, finishing the dabbing at his jacket and tossing the wet towel into the trash.

"Who the hell are *they?*"

"Actually, it's the heart of the offense."

"Screw the offense," Billy said. "Do what you have to do."

"But they have a legitimate chance to repeat this year," Beck said, hoping he could sway his boss just a touch. "I'd really hate to hurt their—"

"Get the damn ring," Billy said. "Do what you have to do."

"I understand," Beck said. He snapped the phone closed, adjusted his suit, and then turned slowly to Rudy.

Rudy only smiled and moved to open the door.

Ten strides later he was down the hall and back in the VIP room.

"Check it out!" Jamil said, his voice carrying over the entire room. "The bitch is back."

15

Beck just strode right at the table of Super Bowl Champion football players. These guys knew how to play ball, but they had no idea how to defend themselves. And just because they were big and strong, they thought they didn't need to learn. It was going to be a lesson Beck wasn't going to enjoy teaching them.

"Why, you mother—"

Knappmiller grabbed a beer bottle off the table and threw it at Beck with the arm that had thrown for more yards last year than any other quarterback's arm had.

The throw was high and just a little wide.

Beck, without missing a stride, reached out and grabbed the bottle out of the air, then sat it on a table as he passed, not missing a step. The bottle had stung his hand when he grabbed it, but he wasn't going to let these bozos know that.

The catch froze the four players for a moment, leaving them standing wide-eyed, and giving Beck one last opening at settling this without a problem.

"I don't want to fight, so I'll ask you for the last time, *give me the ring.*" He spaced out the last four words slow and clear so that even a drunk football player would understand them.

Knappmiller started to move slightly, so Beck went on talking.

"And leave the .38 snub nose in your ankle holster. You don't have a permit and I hate guns. They bring out the worst in everyone."

As Beck had figured, his words did no good. Knappmiller was still standing, stunned that Beck had caught his throw as the other three charged.

The two rookie linemen were lumbering, half-drunk, mountains of flesh, while Jamil was quick and strong. Yet as any good running back, he stayed behind his front line until there was an opening.

Still hoping to not hurt any of them, Beck took the Ohio State grad by the arm as he swung, spun the big man around like a little girl at a dance, and held him with two fingers, showing him to his knees in a shout of extreme pain. A simple twist more and the kid would have trouble with the arm the rest of his life, but Beck made sure that didn't happen.

The other lineman went down a fraction of a second later as Beck took a roundhouse swing and did the same thing to him, sending him to the floor beside his friend.

Jamil seemed to come right at Beck, head on, a fraction of a second behind the two linemen, just like he did in the games when they blocked for him.

Beck stepped sideways, not letting go of the two linemen, and upended the running back with a simple kick.

Then, as Jamil hit the floor hard, square on his back, Beck stepped on his right leg, holding just enough pressure on the leg to cause Jamil a lot of sharp pain, but not enough to break it or do any long-term damage.

With a shout of pain, the running back started to reach for Beck's foot, but Beck pushed down a little harder, forcing Jamil to lie out flat in agony.

Around the quick fight, the VIP room was deadly silent. Only the curses and cries of pain broke the thick air.

Beck held his three captives and looked at the quarterback. The guy was standing beside his table, staring in disbelief.

Actually, Beck hadn't really done anything unusual. The linemen had given him enough time, and Jamil had come in late. Controlling a drunk football player was never a problem if you knew what you were doing.

"I've got a choice of four different bones I can break," Beck said, indicating the three men who were in pain, and making the smart decision to not struggle. "So ask yourself, how many times is Ray Lewis going to smash your head into the turf this year without the best part of your offensive line and no running game to keep him honest?"

"I'm gonna—"

Jamil started to say something and reach for Beck's leg, but again a slight bit more pressure on his leg made him cut his sentence short and gasp in pain.

Knappmiller stared at Beck for a moment, then did exactly what Beck had told him not to do. He reached for his gun and pulled it out.

For Beck, pulling a gun was the worst thing the stupid quarterback could have done.

Suddenly Beck no longer cared about the next season for these idiots.

Suddenly he didn't care what he broke or why.

Beck had been able to control his anger about the Jägermeister in the face, but pulling a gun on him was like taking the pin out of a grenade.

With two quick twists, and a shove with his foot, he sent his three captives into screaming pain, then let them go like they were so much dirty garbage. The next movement they would all make would be on a stretcher.

Before Knappmiller could get the gun up and pointed, Beck was on him, slapping the gun out of Knappmiller's hand.

Then, with all the built-up anger, Beck smashed his fist right into the center of the quarterback's face.

Beck could feel the guy's nose break as the force of his blow sent the quarterback off his feet and flying backward.

With a long stride Beck was over the quarterback, pulling him off the floor by his shirt and pounding him again and again in the face. It was like punching a bag of clothes.

"I told you not to do that!" Beck shouted into the man's bloody face. "Didn't I tell you not to do that?!"

Beck was about to hit the man again, then managed to regain control of himself. Hitting this idiot again would only splatter more blood on his suit, and it was going to be hard enough to clean as it was with all the prune liqueur on it.

Beck dropped the quarterback and straightened up, making sure his jacket was smooth, and the money still in his pocket.

The only noises in the large roomful of people were the moaning and low swearing of the three players, combined with the whimpering of the best quarterback in the world.

"The ring, please," Beck said to Knappmiller.

As the shaking hands of the quarterback managed to pull the ring from his finger, the other players took their rings and tossed them at Beck as well.

Beck took Knappmiller's ring, then turned and headed for the exit. The others could keep their rings. His boss didn't need them for collateral from them. And besides, after what he had just done to them, it was going to be some time, if ever, that they would be getting another, which was too bad for them that they had decided to hang around with a stupid quarterback.

TWO

Beck stepped through the exit and into the dark alley as the noise erupted behind him in the VIP room. More than likely this would hit the news tomorrow, and most of the sports pages around the country, but he didn't care. The stupid idiot had pulled a gun on him, and deserved what he got. Beck had thought Knappmiller might be someone special, but it turned out quarterbacks really were as stupid as everyone said they were, if Knappmiller was the best the league had.

Beck let the big door slam closed behind him and stopped, forcing himself to take a deep breath of the night air and the foul-smelling alley. He didn't like violence, and hated it when people forced him into violent responses. It always took him time to come down from such incidents. He had discovered a year ago that cooking was the best way to make him relax, and ever since his first cooking class it was all he really ever wanted to do.

A second deep breath of the thick, garbage smell of the alley, and the thought of cooking calmed him.

Maybe he should actually try that chef's recipe from the radio. There was no telling what he might be able to do with it once he got his own restaurant open.

He grabbed the small notebook out of his breast pocket and flipped it past different recipes that he had recorded and tried. He had filled dozens of notebooks with recipes over the past few months, and planned on filling more. A cook never knew when the good ones might come in handy.

He flipped to the first blank page, took out a pen, and wrote, *pine nuts, basil, and nutmeg*. Just writing the word nutmeg made him half disgusted. What a stupid thing to put in—

Suddenly a blow to the back of his head sent Beck facedown onto the dirty pavement.

The blow had been hard, and a surprise, but it

hadn't been enough to knock him out, so when he hit, he rolled over, ready to defend himself.

Only a pro could have surprised him like that, and since no one had come out of the emergency door, and no one had come down the alley, whoever had hit him had been waiting for him.

Beck silently cussed his own stupidity. He had stopped and let himself be an easy target instead of moving and making the attacker show himself. A mistake like that, if it didn't get him killed, made him stupid enough to be a quarterback.

A figure stepped forward out of the shadows and loomed over him. It took Beck a moment through the pain to realize who he was looking at.

Martin Hoffler, the biggest man Beck had ever known.

Martin stood over seven feet tall and had shoulders that didn't fit through regular doors. He worked for Billy, Beck's boss.

Martin shouldn't even have been here, let alone be waiting for Beck and hitting him like that.

Of course, the guy was as dumb and mean as he was big, and often hit someone as his way of saying hello. Billy kept him around for the really ugly jobs, and often had to remind the giant man not to kill someone. On more than one occasion, Beck had had to clean up a mess when Billy forgot to remind Martin of that rule.

Martin must have been waiting against the wall, and when Beck had come out of the club figured it was just as safe to hit him as talk. Again, the situation would have been avoided if Beck had just kept moving instead of standing to take a deep breath. He wouldn't make that mistake again.

Beck let himself relax a little and the pain from the blow on his head swept over him even stronger.

"Nice suit," Martin said. "What is that, Armani?"

"Martin," Beck said, the pain worse with the attempt to talk, "what the—"

Martin, acting as if he was going to step forward and help Beck to his feet, instead kicked Beck in the groin.

The pain was so intense that everything went black for a moment.

The next thing Beck knew, Martin was patting him down, finally fishing Knappmiller's Super Bowl ring from Beck's inside pocket. Through the haze of agony Beck watched as Martin held the ring up to the faint light and shook his head.

"Such a violent sport," Martin said, tucking the ring away.

Then whistling a tune Beck didn't recognize, Martin turned away, walking toward the street and finally climbing into a car near the entrance to the alley.

Beck lay there, trying to breathe as deeply as he dared to ease the pain.

He couldn't believe what had just happened. Martin had been there for Billy.

For the ring.

Why?

That was a question Beck wanted answers for.

It took a few long, agonizing minutes, but finally Beck got back to his feet, got his notebook, and managed to get himself back to his pickup.

Twenty minutes later, when he finally pulled his truck into Billy's driveway, the pain had faded some, and he could almost see things clearly.

Almost.

He limped around behind the beautiful estate-size home and through the kitchen door. Billy Walker, an elderly man who controlled a large share of the bookies in the Los Angeles area, was standing at a meat grinder, shoving marinated pork through to make sausage.

Billy looked small and harmless, but anyone who knew him understood how dangerous the man really was. As Knappmiller had discovered, you didn't walk away from Billy Walker.

Billy loved to cook almost as much as Beck did, and Beck had figured that in the kitchen would be where he could find the old man. He had been right.

"There he is," Billy said as Beck pushed through the back door and half-stumbled into the kitchen.

"What was he doing there, Billy?" Beck asked, leaning against the counter and staring at his boss. He could feel the sweat forming on his face now that he had stopped, and he tried to ignore the throbbing pain in both his groin and head.

"You mean Martin?" Billy asked.

Beck said nothing.

"He was backup, that's all. After you called, I wasn't sure you could deliver. Why, what happened?"

"Oh, not much," Beck said, disgusted. "He just hit me with something bigger than a brontosaurus bone, and then kicked me in the balls."

"Jesus," Billy said, staring at Beck, "you want some Advil? I got some Advil somewhere."

Billy left the meat grinder and headed for the drawer on the other side of the counter as Beck moved toward the fridge. As Billy fished in a drawer, Beck pulled out a bag of frozen vegetables and looked at them.

"You know that freezing takes out practically all the vitamins?"

Billy ignored the comment as Beck pressed the bag to the back of his head. For a moment the cold made the pain worse.

Then with the other hand Beck reached out and grabbed the bottle of Advil that Billy tossed.

"They say to take two," Billy said, "but . . ."

Beck poured six or seven Advil directly into his mouth, swallowed, and then grabbed a glass of water and downed the entire glass. It would take a lot more than two to stop this pain. His groin and midsection was going to be black and blue for days, and more than likely he would have a massive headache very soon.

Billy moved over to his old-fashioned Rolodex that sat beside a breadbox on the counter, then pulled a pencil from the drawer. With a quick flip through the cards he pulled one and started writing on it.

"That's ten off your vig, anyway."

"We agreed on twenty," Beck said, trying to make himself stay calm.

"Twenty was for *delivering* me the ring," Billy said. "Letter of the law, champ."

"He stole it from me," Beck said, disgusted.

"Best I can do is fifty-percent split for walkin' it out. Ten grand."

Beck shook his head, immediately sorry that he had. "For what I went through."

Billy put the card back in the file and spread his hands to Beck. "Principle of the thing."

Beck knew that getting angry at Billy wouldn't help anything. He had gotten himself into the position of owing Billy, and no amount of anger was going to get him out.

"You can't keep nickel-and-diming me here, Billy," Beck said, adjusting the bag of frozen vegetables against the large lump on his head. "I've got plans."

"Come on," Billy said, "you go to cooking school for six months, suddenly you're Wolfgang Puck? People like us don't open restaurants, we set fire to them."

Beck wasn't going to allow Billy to sway him. "People change."

And Beck knew he was going to be one of those people, no matter what Billy or anyone else thought.

"Do they?" Billy asked.

He went back to putting the sausage casings onto the end of the meat grinder like slipping a condom on a penis.

Beck said nothing, fighting to get his anger down under his headache.

"You know, it's a tough business, the restaurant business," Billy said as he worked over the grinder. "Seventy-five percent of 'em go under in the first year, and you know why?"

Beck again said nothing. He knew exactly why, but he wasn't going to give Billy any lead.

"*Undercapitalization,*" Billy said. "It takes so much—"

"I want a normal life, Billy," Beck said, keeping his voice low and clear. They had had this conversation before. He wasn't in the mood to have Billy go through all the reasons why Beck couldn't start a restaurant. Eventually Beck would be free and clear of the old man and starting his own restaurant was exactly what he planned on doing.

Billy stared at him for a moment, then wiped his hands on a towel. Beck knew that he had made his point. He was not asking for permission to leave. He was going to leave the moment he was clear of what he owed Billy, and not one second later, no matter how much Billy wanted to keep him around.

Billy gave Beck a look, as if asking if he was sure.

Beck kept his gaze firm into Billy's stare.

He was sure.

Very sure.

"Okay, kid," Billy said, shaking his head and moving to a counter near the door. He opened a drawer and pulled out a manila folder, then stepped forward and handed it to Beck.

Beck glanced at it without opening it. Nothing on the outside at all to give him a hint at what it contained. But he could tell from Billy's movements that this was important to him. Much more than just collecting a bad gambling debt from some football player.

"One job," Billy said, indicating the folder. "One job and your slate's wiped clean. How about it?"

Beck knew better than to commit to something Billy wanted him to do without first knowing what it was, even with the promise of being out from under Billy's thumb.

"Just open it, will ya?" Billy asked, clearly not happy that Beck was hesitating now that he had gone this far.

Beck slipped the clasp and opened the envelope. Inside was a grainy high-altitude or satellite photo of a man. The shot was a pretty good one, considering the distance it had been taken from. Beck could tell the guy in the picture was in his mid-twenties, and was holding a small pick and wearing a miner's hat cocked to one side of his head. The picture was good enough that Beck might even be able to recognize the man if he saw him.

Around the man was a muddy street of some shanty town, clearly not in any part of the world that Beck wanted to visit for its food.

Billy pointed to the picture. "That's a recon photo of Travis Alfred Walker, aspiring archaeologist, Stanford dropout, treasure hunter."

Billy shook his head, clearly disgusted. "To date he's never found anything but trouble."

Beck glanced at Billy, then back at the picture.

"Walker?" He knew Billy had been married a

bunch of times, but there had never been a mention of kids before.

"My son," Billy said. "Third marriage, lasted three minutes."

He made a gesture with both hands in front of his chest. "Tits out to here, an ass like a majorette. She was also certifiable."

Billy seemed disgusted by the memory. He pointed at the picture in Beck's hand. "That was taken two months ago in a gold mining town in the middle of the Amazon. I want him back."

"Why don't you just invite him?" Beck asked. From what he could tell from the picture, the kid was clearly an adult. Young, maybe, but still an adult.

"I did," Billy said. "He doesn't trust me."

Beck laughed, trying to ignore the pain the movement made in his head. "Well, kidnapping ought to help."

Billy stared at Beck for a moment, then clearly decided to tell Beck at least part of the truth. "The kid pissed off the wrong people, champ. I don't need to remind you what happens when you do that, do I?"

Beck refused to take the bait on the problems he had faced when he had angered some certain people. Billy had stepped in and saved him, in his own fashion.

Beck looked down at the photo again, breaking the eye contact with Billy.

"I managed to buy the kid some forgiveness."

Beck understood that very well.

"But if I don't bring him back to face the music . . ." Billy left the sentence hanging because they both knew the likely outcome of that.

Then Billy laughed. "And you know I sure as hell can't carry a tune."

Suddenly it all became clear to Beck why Billy was willing to set Beck free completely with this mission. Billy's life was on the line as well as his son's. Billy had committed the cardinal sin of letting blood get in the way of his judgment, and now he needed Beck to bail him out.

"Deliver him to me in one piece," Billy said, his voice low and controlled, "and you leave my house a free man."

Billy yanked open a drawer and pulled out a stack of large bills. He flipped the bundled stack onto the counter in front of Beck.

"Expenses."

Beck stared at the photo, then leaned over and

took the money off the counter, stuffing it into his suit pocket. One more chore, and then he was done. He didn't much like going to the Amazon to do the chore, but lately he had been in and out of hell right here in Los Angeles, so how much worse could the Amazon be?

"I can smell the risotto in your new place now," Billy said, smiling as he turned to go back to work on the sausage.

Beck watched the old man stuff the sausage casings and wondered why he had such a bad feeling about all this.

THREE

Travis Walker crouched on the roof of the old guard shack on the edge of the Global Gold Corporation mining site. Around him was hot Amazon jungle, with only a wide dirt road leading through it to the mining area. Why Global had put the guard station here was anyone's guess, since someone trying to get onto the property could just go through the jungle unseen.

But considering everything that lurked in that jungle, it might be safer to just face the guards.

Leaning forward, Travis studied as best he could the two guards inside through a side window. Both wore sweat-stained brown uniforms and carried pistols on their hips. From the look of their shirts and greasy hair, neither had bathed in a week. Travis could just imagine the smell inside that shack. He was glad to be up on the roof, even though if they caught him, they would shoot him and ask what he was doing later.

But he didn't plan on getting caught. He was just here to make a little trade.

One guard sat in a tattered chair facing a small television. He was drinking a beer, and from what Travis could tell of his uniform, he was in charge. From the sideways glance at the grainy picture, the guard was trying to watch *Jeopardy!* When Travis found himself watching that show he always shouted out the answers ahead of the contestants. This guard wasn't saying anything, more than likely because he didn't even pretend to know any answers.

The junior of the two guards stood in the front doorway to the shedlike building, spitting coca juice in long streams onto a fallen TRESPASSERS WILL BE SHOT sign. This guy had a nasty-looking scar and seemed to be the type that would shoot you just for the fun of it. Global Gold tended to hire men like him, especially for these jungle guard stations.

Travis took a deep breath, wiped the sweat from his forehead, and looked back at the small satellite dish near the peak of the roof. He was going to have to make the switch quickly, or they would see him for sure.

He moved silently up the roof to the dish and settled in a position on the back side of the building, letting the ridge of the roof work as a partial shelter in case anyone came out the front door to go take a leak or something.

Then he took out a portable DVD player from his pouch and checked to make sure it was working. In this kind of Amazon heat and humidity, you were always better served to check any equipment before using it. In the jungle, electronics seemed to not last very long.

Finally he retrieved the jewel case containing the movie that he had brought with him, and stared at the three mostly naked women on the cover.

Spice VII—Sinful Sisters.

Travis had no doubt that if he could make the switch fast enough, the sisters in this artful movie would more than keep the two guards occupied long enough for him to get what he came here for.

He slipped the movie into place and started the DVD player, letting it run long enough to get past the opening credits and into the action of the movie, such as the "action" was in a movie titled *Sinful Sisters*. Then with a swift cut of the knife that he kept tucked in his belt, he cut the cable leading from the satellite dish to the small television below.

"*Porra!*" the guard inside near the television shouted as the image went out. "*O kue kue esta——?*"

Travis heard the other guard mutter something, spit, and turn from the doorway.

Quickly Travis spliced in the DVD to the cable leading to the television, making sure the DVD player was still running.

"Antenna!" one of the guards said.

"Come on, baby," Travis whispered, finishing the last splice that finished hooking the wire up to the running DVD player. Then he sat holding his breath, staring at the front edge of the roof to make sure no guard appeared.

"*Meu Deus!*" one guard said.

Travis smiled. The sisters had come through for him, clearly, and in all their naked glory.

"Okay," Travis whispered to himself, "let's see what the rest of the world is doing."

He pulled his laptop from his pouch and quickly worked with the end of the cable that went to the satellite dish, opening the cable and making a connection that would work with his laptop. He had done this a dozen times before, so he was getting fast at it.

Then, after the wire was secure, with a few quick taps on the computer, he sent for his e-mail.

"C'mon, baby," Travis said. "Give me those three little words."

A moment later the words he had been hoping for came from his laptop. *"You've got mail."*

"Yes," Travis said, a little too loud.

He glanced at the edge of the roof, but no guard was in sight. Clearly the three sisters were keeping them very entertained, and neither had a brain big enough to question where the clear picture was coming from, or why the sharp questions of Alex Trebek had been replaced by the low moaning of three women.

He had a number of e-mail's, including a bunch of spam. Most of the messages were only text, but one struck him and he quickly selected it, downloading it and the files it contained into the memory of the computer as he did. It was the message he was risking his life on this roof to get.

The video e-mail flickered into place on his computer, showing the face of one of his professors from Stanford. Even though the old man had been a jerk, Travis had liked him, and had kept him up on his different adventures, at least the ones that were inside the law.

"Mr. Walker," the professor said, smiling at him through the jerky e-mail transmission, "always a pleasure to hear from one of my most promising students, no matter how brief his academic career."

Travis had known he was going to get a lecture from the old man when he sent the professor his question. Now he smiled at the fact that he was right.

"I must compliment you on your most recent choice of wild goose—"

"Condescending bastard," Travis said, shaking his head fondly as he slid the task bar forward to get to a later part of the message.

"I want to remind you," the professor said, shaking his head, "that the Gato do Diabo is a myth, Travis. No more real than the Shroud of Turin or the Easter Bunny."

If they had been face-to-face Travis would have kidded him about dashing his dreams about hunting down the Easter Bunny. Just the thought of the conversation made Travis smile.

"The hieroglyphics you sent me were impossibly obscure."

"Damn," Travis said, softly. He had hoped the professor would manage to do something with them.

The professor went on. "Still, I did manage to translate them."

Travis leaned in close to the small screen on the laptop.

"As you no doubt anticipated, they form . . ."

"A map?" Travis asked under his breath.

"A map," the professor said, his face smug.

"Holy shit!" Travis said, closing his eyes for a moment to think about the riches that were just around the corner.

Suddenly one of the guards shouted, *"Porra! Gringo!"*

A bullet screamed over Travis's head, far too close for comfort. The sound of the gunshot seemed to rock the small shack under him.

The DVD player had a red light blinking, meaning the battery was low and the disk had stopped playing. The three sisters were no longer doing their job.

Now both guards were raising their guns to fire at him again.

Leaving the DVD player hooked up, he grabbed his laptop and rolled away from the top of the roof as two more shots cut into the roof where he had been.

With a running jump he hit the dirt behind the shack and rolled, protecting the laptop with both arms as he did so.

"Stop!" one guard shouted.

Like he was going to stop so they could get a clear shot? Not likely.

Travis came up out of the roll running toward the edge of the jungle.

Another shot echoed through the jungle and dust kicked up just in front of him.

Too damn close for comfort.

He got to the edge of the thick green foliage, ducked low, and then went directly right along the edge of the cleared road as the guards kept firing into the deep green. He wasn't stupid enough to run headlong into the jungle.

He went fifty paces down the edge of the road, staying in the thick green underbrush, then stopped as the guards, still firing, decided to dive into the jungle to chase him.

Travis shook his head and stepped back out into the open, listening to the shots and swearing as the two went deeper into the Amazon. They were so stupid they would be lucky to find their way back out again.

He tucked the laptop back in his pouch, climbed quickly back up on the roof and retrieved the DVD player and the three sisters. There was no telling when they would come in handy again.

Then whistling, he headed off down the road, the sounds of the two guards now only distant swearing in the dense, thick jungle.

FOUR

Beck felt as if he'd been traveling forever. When he had accepted the assignment from Billy, he had had no real idea about the vast distances from Los Angeles to Brazil. He had just never given it a moment's thought until he got his plane ticket.

The first flight had lasted what had seemed like a lifetime, mostly because he was crammed into a space where his knees jammed against the magazine pouch on the back of the seat in front of him and his hips were pinched against the armrests. Airline seats just weren't made for a man his size.

By the time the plane left the ground he wished he had spent some of Billy's money for a first class ticket. But he had figured he would fly as cheaply as possible and save the money for his restaurant.

So instead he jammed himself into the small seat and read food magazines.

To make matters worse, the man in the seat in front of him smelled bad, like ten-day-old sweat-socks. The guy had leaned his seat back when the flight took off and started snoring. He had only put the seat back up when asked at the end of the flight. Not even focusing on receipts and the lay-out of the restaurant Beck hoped to build could overcome ten hours of looking at the greasy top of the man's head.

As he limped off the plane before the sun even came up, wondering if feeling would ever return to his legs, he swore he would spend the extra money going back and fly first class, no matter the cost.

On the second leg of the trip into the Amazon, Beck had taken something laughingly called an airline to a smaller airport in a town with a name he couldn't pronounce. The plane was so small it only had eight seats, and Beck had to almost crawl on his hands and knees to reach his seat because the ceiling was so low.

The flight had been bumpy and blissfully short compared to the one before. He had consid-ered himself lucky to be on the ground after that flight, considering that the seats had holes in them and the carpet was worn clear through to the metal in many places. He could only imagine how well the engines were kept up.

After the second flight he had grabbed a quick breakfast at a place with another name he couldn't pronounce and had food that was far too spicy for his tastes. Then he had gone back to the airport.

And now, for the third and final leg of the trip, he was in the passenger seat of a plane that seemed to be far too small to even fly, and far too old to hold together. It also had the loudest engine he had ever been near. He had to hunch over just to keep his head from banging on the roof.

From the first moment the plane bounced twice on the runway and finally left the ground, he had felt airsick, and the gas and oil smell that filled the tiny cabin didn't help.

Now, after twenty of the longest minutes of his life, he held a small white bag in one hand while trying not to touch any of the instruments or controls in front of him with the other.

The pilot of the plane, Declan Farrel, had said his was the only real transportation into the gold mining town where Travis Walker had been spotted, unless Beck planned to take a two-day truck ride through the jungle on bad roads. Beck had almost gone for the truck ride, and was now wishing he had.

Declan Farrel also had claimed he was the best pilot south of the Panama Canal. More than likely he was one of the only pilots. He was as Irish as they come, short, and very stout. He had started calling Beck "little fella" the moment he saw him, and no matter how much Beck glared at the small man, Declan wouldn't stop.

Now that Declan had leveled the plane off at some sort of cruising altitude over the vast Amazon jungle, he dug into a bag beside his seat and pulled out a bologna-and-mayo sandwich, offering part of it to Beck.

The smell choked the small cockpit, even managing to cover the oil and gas odor for a moment. Beck managed to not lose what little bit of breakfast he had.

Declan only shrugged at Beck's hand-waving decline and started into the sandwich.

Beck tried not to watch as the small Irishman kept working at his food no matter how much the plane dipped and seemed to want to fall from the sky.

After one rather large jerk and dip, Beck

opened the white bag, but somehow managed to not use it. Another dip like that one and he wasn't going to be so lucky.

Declan laughed, then shouted over the roar of the engine, "Don't worry, little fella, she may be old and ugly, but she's always up for a toss."

Beck had no idea exactly what Declan was talking about, and at this point he didn't care. He turned his head away from the eating pilot and stared out at the wing of the small plane and the expanse of green jungle below. For a moment he wasn't sure what he was seeing, then it became clear. The skin of the wing was patched in a number of places.

"Is that duct tape?" Beck asked, pointing out the window.

"Ay," Declan shouted back between chews.

"I'm serious," Beck said, turning to stare at the pilot to make sure his voice was heard over the roaring of the engine. "Is that duct tape?"

The feeling that he might actually be in danger of losing his life started to ease up over the feeling of airsickness, and it had been years since even a slight bit of fear had bothered Beck.

"Ay," the pilot said, finishing off the last of the sandwich as the plane lurched forward and down.

"Steady yourself, little fella. Walk by faith, not by sight."

Beck was about to tell the old Irishman what he thought of that idea when the plane's nose suddenly pointed at the ground, as if someone had just taken it and shoved downward.

"Whoa!" Declan shouted, laughing as he fought the controls like a kid on a ride at the fair. "Hold onto your lunch."

Somehow Beck managed to not lose the very upset contents of his stomach as the pilot got the plane leveled again, albeit at a much lower altitude than before. Beck figured that somehow the human body didn't let a person throw up just before they were about to die. And during that dive Beck had sworn he was going to die.

"There she festers," Declan shouted to him as if the sudden drop they had been through was an everyday occurrence. Declan pointed ahead and off to Beck's right.

Beck forced his attention past the duct-taped wing at the huge brown area coming up at them. It was as if a giant scoop had just ripped the jungle from the ground, leaving nothing but brown rocks and dirt.

"You're lookin' at four years of nonstop gobble, gobble!" Declan shouted over the engine. "They suck the Earth dry and give 'er no mercy. Biggest gold mine on the planet!"

Beck couldn't believe what he was seeing. The small plane was still over the jungle, yet the vast open sore in the green landscape seemed to go on forever in front of them.

"How big is it?"

"About two miles wide!" Declan shouted. "Four thousand men digging in the dirt with their claws. An evil trade is plied there, alright!"

Beck stared out the plane's window for a moment, his stomach leaving him alone now that he had something else to focus on.

From this distance and height, he could see massive piles of rock and dirt. Paths and roads twisted and wound their way through the area with no seeming pattern. A few trucks kicked up dust clouds behind them. Even from a few thousand feet in the air Beck could see the tiny dots of men moving around, sometimes blending completely in with the dirt.

"Who runs the show down there?" Beck asked over the motor noise.

"The show?" Declan asked, clearly not understanding.

"The boss?" Beck said.

"Oh," Declan said, shaking his head as if the question disgusted him. "That would be Cornelius Hatcher, head of the corporation's mining company."

Declan glanced to his left and then banked the plane hard, dropping altitude as he did.

Beck managed to hold on to the window and his white airsickness bag as Delcan went on shouting over the loud engine.

"Hatcher's a charmin' fella, too. Buy you a drink and make you eat the bloody glass."

Declan leveled the plane out and ahead Beck could see a runway cut from the jungle. It looked to be at least three miles from the main area of the mine, and a few miles from a clearing that held some buildings.

"First time in El Dorado, is it, Mr. Beck?" Declan asked, for the first time not calling Beck "little fella."

"Yeah," Beck said, not happy with the way the plane was drifting back and forth and up and down while the runway in front of them seemed very stable and very, very hard, even though it was covered in grass.

"Did you bring your Bible?" Declan asked.

Beck glanced at the small Irishman beside him, but it was clear the guy was serious. He was about to ask Declan what he meant when something ahead caught his attention. On the runway was a large herd of cattle.

He pointed, and was about to shout a warning, when it became clear that Declan had no intention of landing the plane into those cattle. But he *was* going to buzz the runway at an near-impossible low level.

Beck watched as best he could out the side window as the plane dipped below the level of the Amazon trees and skimmed over the runway. The herd of cattle scattered under the close fly-over of the plane but didn't leave the runway. It seemed to Beck that they were so low that the wheels of the plane must have grazed the cattle's backs.

Beck glanced back to see what kind of effect they had had in clearing the cattle as Declan pulled the nose of the plane up to miss the tops of the trees at the end of the runway. Suddenly a black dog streaked from near a small building beside the runway and started to herd the cattle even farther out of the way, nipping at their heels to make them move faster.

Declan banked around hard, the jungle seemingly only a few feet from the duct-taped wing. Then he leveled out and, before Beck could even take a breath to recover, bounced the small plane onto the runway.

The plane skipped and skidded on the rough surface, then the tail dropped, bouncing once before it settled down. From there the landing felt more like a rough car ride as Declan veered left to miss a few of the slower cattle.

Beck felt his stomach ease at just the thought of being on the ground.

Declan steered the plane off the runway, across what looked like nothing but open pasture, and finally to a halt near the lone building.

Beck could not believe he had survived that ride. He sat panting as the engines died, leaving them in a silence so loud it made his ears ring.

A number of men and women came from near the building and walked toward them. From what Beck could tell they looked like a cross between Inca and Spanish. They wore light clothes with bright colors that covered most of their skin, and all but one woman had on a wide-brimmed hat.

Declan climbed from his side of the plane and

dropped to the ground, saying something to the closest man, which Beck couldn't hear.

The thick, hot air of the jungle washed into the plane, making Beck sweat even more. It was still early in the morning and already very hot. Beck didn't want to think about how hot it would be in the middle of the afternoon. And he had no intention of finding out. He was going to get Walker and get out.

It took Beck a few moments later to unwind his bulk and get out on the other side. The ground felt wonderful, and he stopped and took a deep breath, resisting the impulse to just sit down on the grass and weeds and celebrate that he was still alive. His stomach was going to take some time to settle, but at least he had managed to get this far without losing any lunch.

He straightened his jacket and brushed off his pants. He had picked a light-colored suit that resisted wrinkles and an open shirt for this trip, and right now he was glad he had.

Around him the tall trees and brush of the jungle lined the runway, making it feel like it was a room without a ceiling. So this was the last known place of Travis Walker. Why on Earth would anyone come here?

He grabbed his small shoulder bag, his only luggage, and moved around the plane to join Declan and the others as they started to unload the plane's cargo hold.

"Nice work, Bones," Declan said, tossing the huge, black sheepdog a biscuit where it lay panting in the shade of the plane. "Well done."

Beck started to lean down to pet the dog when Declan said, "I wouldn't do that if I were you, friend. This one's a killer."

Beck smiled at Declan, but the small Irishman didn't smile back, so Beck pulled back his hand slowly and stepped away from the dog, who didn't seem to even notice him.

"This way," Declan said, turning toward the building as the locals worked to unload the full cargo hold of the airplane.

With one quick glance back at the panting dog, Beck followed.

Out of sight from where they had landed was an open-topped Jeep that looked well used and a few years old. Beck stashed his bag behind the passenger seat and climbed in as Declan fired up the engine and jerked them down a narrow, muddy road cut through the jungle.

The green jungle that seemed to want to swallow the road looked too thick to even walk through, and the air, in spite of with the breeze from the speeding Jeep, was heavy and getting warmer by the minute. "Oppressive" was all Beck could think to call the feeling around him.

"This the only road in and out?" Beck asked Declan, again slightly shouting over the engine and wind noise.

"If you wanna stay alive," Declan said, not taking his eyes off of the road ahead.

"How's that?"

Declan pointed at the green thickness that towered over the road on both sides. "That there is the jungle, little fella. You got anacondas, poison-arrow frogs, black flies, bullet ants, jumpin' spiders, malaria, typhoid, ochuba, and man-eating jaguars, just to name a few."

Beck stared at the Irishman, who laughed and went on. "And if all of that don't get ya, the rebels will."

"Rebels?" Beck asked, kicking himself for not studying up even more on the local political situation. "Fighting the government?"

"No government," Declan said, shaking his head. "They're fighting the devil himself. Cornelius Hatcher's mine is the hold of every foul spirit and the cage of every unclean and hateful bird."

Beck was about to ask what exactly Declan meant when the Irishman took his eyes off the road long enough to stare at Beck.

"Sunday school picnic is over. Stay out of the jungle, little fella."

A moment later they broke out of the narrow road and into an area where the jungle had been cut back farther. Ahead Beck could see buildings of some sort.

A bullet-riddled sign was propped beside the road. At one point it had said EL DORADO. But someone had painted over the first part of the word with the word HELL.

Hell Dorado.

This wasn't going to be like marching into a nightclub and taking a football player's ring, that was for sure.

Declan slowed the Jeep as they reached the outskirts of the town, such as it was. Beck slowly took in every detail.

The mud street up the center, rutted and rough.

The wood and corrugated tin buildings, most with only small windows that were shuttered and had no glass.

Stripped logs stuck into the ground every fifty paces like telephone poles, only instead of wires, mounted on each was a high-tech security camera. Every move made in this town was watched by someone.

Burned-out cars, stripped of any useful part, littered areas between buildings and along the road. The town looked more like a war zone than a place where people lived.

Miners, covered in brown mud with only their eyes and mouths showing, passed the Jeep in industrial-size trucks, going somewhere into the jungle.

The people on the rough boards that served as walkways between the buildings walked slowly, keeping their eyes focused on the ground in front of them, as if looking up was dangerous and just too much work.

Beck had no doubt after one quick look at this town why someone thought this place hell.

Another large truck full of miners roared past them as Declan moved the Jeep out of the way.

Declan nodded at the miners. "They work six twelve-hour days a week in one-hundred-and-twelve-degree heat. Their water's rationed. They put up with daily strip searches where the man checks your ass and your teeth with the same hand."

Declan spit out the side of the Jeep, clearly disgusted. "Hatcher pays each ten dollars, if they're lucky, so that they can come down here to Hatcher's town and pay a buck for a bar of soap at Hatcher's store, or two for a beer at his bar."

Declan shook his head as they kept moving through town, heading for the bigger buildings on the far side.

"The devil's in the details," Declan said.

From what Beck could see, Declan was right.

FIVE

Travis adjusted his clean shirt, making sure it was tucked in neatly. A clean shirt in this place was something to be savored and protected for as long as possible. Nothing ever stayed clean with all the mud and heat, so when he managed to get a clean shirt, and his jeans clean as well, it was a special day.

With luck, today would be very special.

He put the fistful of flowers he had picked from the jungle earlier this morning behind his back, then stepped through the front door of the El Piedra saloon and into the dark, slightly cooler, interior. He had been both dreading, and looking forward to, this moment since he had gotten the e-mail from his old professor. His stomach twisted. So much rode on his ability to get the right answer very soon.

The place was almost empty of customers, as Travis had expected it to be. This time of the day almost everyone was working the mine, getting in their time before it got too hot. There were only a few helpless drunks sprawled on the tables, and three corporate security types playing dominoes in the back.

Mariana was behind the bar, slowing wiping down the surface. Travis stood and just watched as her dark hair flowed around her face like a waterfall hiding her beauty, then revealing it, then hiding it again. Her eyes were dark and intense, her lips full, with just a slight touch of lipstick.

This morning she wore a white blouse with peasant sleeves that accented her wonderful body, a body that Travis hoped to someday get much, much closer to.

She glanced up and saw him standing there, staring at her.

He stepped forward and extended the bright blue-and-orange-flecked flowers in his hand. "I found these growing in the deepest part of the jungle."

Actually, he'd only found them by a stream about a mile away, but the deepest part sounded better, more impressive. And he had no doubt she believed he was stupid enough to go into the deepest parts of the jungles around here just to pick flowers.

"As far as I can tell," he said, going on, "no one's ever identified them."

He hadn't even looked them up, so that was a sort of stretching things. But since he actually had no way of knowing, he wasn't completely lying. He honestly couldn't tell what they were called, or if they had ever been seen by anyone before.

"That means I'm responsible for naming this flower, and I can only think of one word, one sound that fits something so beautiful."

He thrust the flowers toward her.

"Mariana," he said. "I'm calling them Mariana."

She didn't take the flowers, but instead stared into his eyes. "How much do you want?"

"I am crushed," Travis said, putting the flowers on the bar as if they were delicate glass. "Wounded. Can't a fellow crave the company of a beautiful—"

She stared at him. "How much?"

He had no doubt at that moment that this was going to be a lot harder than he had imagined it would be.

"Not a cent," he said, holding out his hands as

if he had his left hand on an invisible Bible and his right hand in the air and were about to testify in court. "I swear. On my life, I swear."

She stared at him, not letting their gazes break apart. She knew him far too well, and was far too smart for him to try to trick her. The only way he was going to get what he needed was to tell her the truth.

"Just if I could borrow your uncle's boat. I'm talking a day or two, max."

Mariana shook her head and sighed, then walked away from him and the flowers, moving to clean a couple tables in the corner.

She was so beautiful. Usually he would just stand and watch her move, but now he had something very important to do and he needed that boat to make it safely to where he had to go.

"Mariana, listen," he started to say.

She spun on him, her black eyes blazing in anger. "No, *you* listen. First my car and you bring it back with no windshield."

He had to admit that hadn't been the best way to return her car. But where was he going to get a windshield fixed in the middle of the jungle?

"Then it was my brother's scooter. That one you don't bring back at all."

It would have been tough to get from the bottom of the river, considering what lived in that river, but he didn't say anything. He had learned that with Mariana, when she was ranting, it was better to just let her get it all out.

"Now you want my uncle's boat. What next? My sister's baby carriage? And each time it's *'I have found it! I have found it!'* You will never find it, this 'Garbo.' "

"Shhh," Travis said, glancing around to see if anyone had heard her. No one had noticed, and the few drunks who were in the bar wouldn't have cared anyway.

"It's 'Gato,' " he said, keeping his voice low.

"Like I say." She waved him off and went to scrubbing a table top.

Travis moved around to a point where he could talk directly to her. He was going to have to level with her completely to make this work. "Francisco Córdova. Pedro Olerra. They wrote about it in 1544."

"So," she said, not looking up at him.

"They saw it with their own eyes before the Marajo Indians hid it for good."

This time she said nothing, so he went on.

"It's out there, Mariana. I'm not guessing this

65

time. I know exactly where it is and I'm going to get it. But I need that boat."

Mariana glanced up at him and held his gaze. She could tell, he knew. She could tell just by looking at him that he was telling the truth. She always had a way of cutting through all his bull.

Finally, after a long moment, she asked, "How much?"

"I told you—"

"No, how much is your Gato worth?"

Now he understood what she was after. "Oh, money." He shook his head. "Not worth that much money. It's more of an academic find, really."

She laughed. "You lie like a little girl, Travis."

She reached out and touched his cheek. The feel of her hand against his skin sent chills down his back and made him sweat into his clean shirt.

"I get you boat," she said, rubbing her hand along his face as if trying to seduce him. "You take me with you."

"Now, Mariana," he said softly, hoping she wouldn't move her hand away.

But she did, looking with her dark eyes into his. "We split the take fifty-fifty."

"We're talking a lousy boat, here," he said, now really worried. She had no idea how much money she was asking for. Her half would buy a thousand yachts if they found the thing.

She shrugged and went back to wiping off the table, making him wish he as the water-stained wooden top the way her hand moved in circles, stroking the cloth over the surface.

"I'm off at six," she said, without looking up at him. "Then we go get your Gato."

The day was getting warmer and stickier by the minute, already hotter and more humid than the worst summer day in Los Angeles. Declan had driven him through the town, such as it was, and then doubled back, taking him to see Hatcher at the mine.

Ahead of the Jeep now was a sight Beck could only imagine in his worst nightmares. Two, side-by-side high-wire fences went off over the cleared land at ninety-degree angles from the road, looking like double-thick walls of a fort. Beck knew that inside the fences was the two-mile-wide gold mine he had seen from the air. But from where he sat it looked more like a prison than a mine.

At the inside fence a long line of mud-crusted miners waited in single file that lead through a gate and to a small shack. Behind the shack was a two-story building that sat between the fences, protected from both the outside world and the inside world of the mine at the same time.

The shack looked to be some sort of pay station and had two guards standing beside it. Other guards were stationed around the building and along the road. The pay window was covered in a kind of cage, like a gas station attendant would have back in Los Angeles. The guards nearest the station had both sidearms and nasty-looking whips. Beck had no doubt they both knew how to use each weapon.

Declan nodded in the direction of a man who paced near the shack, barking orders as he walked. Declan had described the man named Harvey perfectly to Beck earlier. Harvey was short and looked mean, like a pit bull. He was Hatcher's brother and second in command. Beck was going to have to get through him first to get to Hatcher.

Declan went through one guard checkpoint and parked the Jeep off to one side of the road near a couple of trucks. He took the keys, and then, walking beside Beck, they headed toward the entrance to hell.

Just as they reached the gate opening one guard barked something in Portuguese that Beck didn't understand.

Declan turned to Beck. "He wants to know if you carry a gun."

"Tell him no," Beck said, raising his arms to let his jacket fall open to show no holster under his arm. "I don't like them."

Declan shrugged and did as he was told, speaking back to the guard in what seemed like a very strange language coming from the Irishman's mouth.

The guard answered and Declan laughed, turning to Beck. "He said he never met an American who doesn't like guns."

Beck only shrugged.

Declan glanced up and shouted. "Hey, Harvey!"

Harvey turned and stared at them through the fence. Beck couldn't tell if the guy didn't like Declan or just never smiled. Beck would have bet on the second choice.

"Got one to see your brother," Declan shouted through the fence, nodding at Beck.

None of the clearly exhausted miners seemed to pay any attention at all, either to Beck or to the conversation.

"What's your business?" Harvey asked, moving over to stand in front of Beck at the gate.

"My business is with your brother," Beck said, staring into the cold, dead eyes of the short man.

It was clear to Beck that this man would rather kill a person than talk to him. If push ever came to shove, Beck would need to deal with Harvey first. He just hoped it didn't come down to that.

Harvey finally nodded, then quickly frisked Beck, doing a quick, professional job that wouldn't have missed much of anything.

Then, motioning that Declan should stay with the Jeep, Harvey turned and led Beck into the larger building and up a flight of stairs to an observation deck that looked out over the scarred earth called a mine.

Beck could tell that every inch of the gate, the road, and the building were monitored with high-tech cameras. This Hatcher took no chances, that much was clear.

Inside the second floor of the building was a large room that was air-conditioned, making Beck break out into a sweat before the door was closed behind him.

The room looked more like a command central for a space mission than a mine security control area. One entire wall was filled by monitors, constantly moving from camera to camera as three men sat in front of them, monitoring each picture.

Computers filled every spare space, and near

the center of the room were glass layouts of the mine, divided into zones and marked on with grease markers of different colors.

In a large chair that swiveled, placed in the middle of the room on a raised platform, sat Cornelius Hatcher. He was wearing a Kevlar vest and at the moment was focused on one of the glass displays.

"What's the current payout?" Hatcher demanded of a man sitting at a control station near one board.

The man tapped what looked like a communications button, or maybe an intercom to another area of the building. "Give me the payout at quadrant three."

"Two-four to -five," a voice came back. "Down ten percent."

Hatcher shook his head. "Well, tell them to dig harder."

Then Hatcher swung around to face Beck. Hatcher's thin, weathered face gave off a sense of power and control and intellect. This man was used to getting his way, of that Beck had no doubt.

"If only it were that simple," Hatcher said, staring into Beck's eyes, "eh, Mr. Beck?"

"How do you know my name?" Beck asked,

keeping his voice flat and without threat, not showing the surprise he felt.

Hatcher smiled but didn't laugh. "I have rebels in the jungle and a price on my head." He tapped the bullet-proof vest he wore. "When a man of your dimensions travels all that way to visit a place like this . . ." Hatcher paused, then smiled and continued, "Shall we say it aroused the curiosity."

Beck nodded and pulled the folded satellite photo of Travis from his pocket. He opened it and stepped forward to hand it to Hatcher.

"Do you know this man?"

Hatcher glanced at the photo, then handed it back to Beck who put it back in his jacket.

"Ah, Trav-ass," Hatcher said, almost spitting out the words. "I let him do some excavating around the mine, in the jungle and such. I allow him to rent a room in my town. All in the exchange for a fair sixty percent of anything he might unearth."

Beck didn't want to comment on how fair it all sounded. "Can you tell me where to find him?"

"Just listen for the bullshit," Harvey said, not hiding the fact that Travis had gotten under his skin. It seemed the kid could do that. Beck had gotten the same sense from his father.

Harvey shook his head. "The guy's got a mouth should be in the circus."

"Brother, please," Hatcher said, holding up his hand for Harvey to stop. Then Hatcher turned to Beck, his face serious. "Do you have business with him?"

"It's personal," Beck said, again keeping his voice flat and without threat.

"So why come to me?" Hatcher asked.

"When you're a guest in another man's home," Beck said, keeping his gaze locked on Hatcher's, "you don't reach into the refrigerator without his permission."

Hatcher smiled and chuckled. "Come here, Mr. Beck."

Hatcher stood and led Beck to the edge of a deck looking out over the mine. The scar in the earth looked even more dramatic up close. Beck could clearly see the main hole surrounded by vast mounds of dirt. Hundreds, if not thousands of natives were digging in the mud and rock as far as Beck could see.

"Does this look like a refrigerator?" Hatcher asked, waving his arm in the direction of the mine.

Beck stared out at the mine. "Sir, and I mean no offense, this place looks like I've imagined hell."

Again Hatcher chuckled. "Where you see hell, I see a spellbinding sense of purpose. I see opportunity. I see business. I see work."

Beck said nothing, letting Hatcher go on as he pointed to Beck's shirt. "I see what you're wearing, Mr. Beck. Children so small . . . fingers to the bone in Southeast Asia."

He indicated Beck's trousers. "Women working in Beijing sweatshops sixteen hours a day. If that's the price of your meager threads, at what costs come the sublime?"

Beck, at that point, wasn't sure where Hatcher was heading, but he had a hunch the man was going to get to his point soon enough.

In front of them natives climbed up and down ladders that went down into the huge pit, carrying baskets filled with mud and rock. Other men carried dirt up to women running a type of heavy sorting machine.

"When a bride slips the ring on her finger," Hatcher said, staring out over his mine as if he were a god surveying his creation, "when a businessman lays his hand on a Rolex, when a rapper gets a shiny new tooth, this is the cost, Mr. Beck. My horror for their beauty; my hell for their little slice of heaven."

Beck said nothing. He wondered how often Hatcher went to sleep at night justifying what he did to people with this speech. From the looks of what was spread out in front of Beck in the mine, the cost of life here was high. Very high.

Hatcher sighed. "Supply and demand can be a terrible thing. For those of us bold enough to face the cold-eyed fact of life, there can be tremendous reward."

Hatcher turned back toward his command chair, talking as he went. "So what do you want with the kid?"

"I've come to take him home."

"That will cost you ten thousand dollars," Hatcher said.

Beck had a hunch that something like this was coming. He reached into his inside pocket and pulled out a roll of bills. Then he pealed off ten big ones, and before giving them to Hatcher, he extended his hand.

"A handshake is my bond."

Hatcher looked at Beck's hand for a moment, then reached forward and shook it. The man's grip was firm but not too strong.

Hatcher took the money, then said, "Try the local watering hole. He has a Jones for the bartender."

Beck nodded and without another word turned and left, hearing Harvey follow him down the stairs as he went. Outside the fence, Declan leaned against the Jeep, waiting.

"I need the wheels," Beck said as he came up to Declan.

"Now hang on there, mate," Declan said.

"It's worth ten Ben Franklins if you find your own way back to the plane and keep the engine running."

Declan motioned that the Jeep was Beck's and stood aside.

Beck climbed in behind the wheel and then before starting it, turned to Declan, seeing Harvey watching in the background near the entrance.

"Oh, and Declan," Beck said, motioning the Irishman closer.

"Yeah, boss?" Declan asked.

"I may be coming fast."

Declan only nodded and turned away.

A moment later Beck had the Jeep headed down the road back toward the small town. He figured that a man like Declan could find another quick way back to the airport, and would easily be there and waiting by the time Beck found Travis and got him out of the bar.

SIX

Beck slid the Jeep to a stop in the mud in front of the largest building in the small town. The bar, with a faded sign, was built of wood and it looked as if no one had ever bothered to paint it. A wooden sidewalk of planks in front allowed Beck to not have to step into the drying mud when climbing from the Jeep.

The late-morning air was now so thick and humid, it felt as if it wrapped around Beck's face and hands, pushing him down. And it got a lot warmer in the afternoon, from what he understood. How anyone lived here was a mystery to him. It made the hottest summer day in Los Angeles seem like a cold arctic wind.

The bar's front door was wide open, and the

inside was darker than the bright day. Beck
stepped through the door and sideways to get out
of the light coming in the door behind him. It
took a moment of standing beside a table before
his eyes adjusted.

An old Indian woman pushed a mop while
two drunks lay with their heads down on tables.
Beck studied each to make sure that both were
really what they appeared to be. The only other
occupants of the bar were two men in the back
corner playing dominoes, slamming the cup on
the table with a bang every fifteen seconds. Both
looked like they were guards for the corporation,
and no doubt carried weapons.

Beck moved over to the bar and sat down as a
very attractive young woman in a white blouse
came through a curtain from a room off to the
left. She had long, dark hair and dark eyes that
could cut through steel. It was no wonder
Hatcher had said that Travis had a thing for this
woman. It would be easy to do. She was about as
beautiful as they came, and Beck was used to a
Southern California level of beautiful woman.

Beck stared at her as she walked toward him
along the front of the bar, wiping her hands on a
towel tucked into the belt of her jeans. The

motion was one of a longtime bartender. He knew she had checked him over for danger by the way her eyes looked at him without really focusing on any one area. And there was a street-smart look in those eyes that he liked.

"American?" she asked, her voice full and rich and showing her intelligence even more.

She stopped a few feet from him and stared back. She had put just enough of an accent on the word to make someone not sure of her history.

"Hmmm," he said, not really answering her question because he knew there was no need to. She had him figured, more than likely down to the area of Los Angeles he was from.

"Where about?" she asked. Again, she added what was clearly a local twang to her words.

He stared into her dark eyes for a moment, then said, "Somewhere they have bartenders."

She shrugged, turned her back on him, and moved around the end of the bar, stopping to face him over the wooden surface. She slid a blank paper coaster in front of him with a practiced motion. "What can I get you?"

Now he smiled. Her gaze was even harder, more intent on figuring him out.

"What do the locals drink?"

She laughed, the sound more intoxicating than any liquor this bar could serve. "Anything they can."

"I'll take a beer," Beck said.

She bent over and grabbed a beer glass from under the bar, then started to pull the beer off the tap.

"Nice flowers," Beck said, indicating the vaseful on the back bar.

She slid the beer in front of him. *"O tolo sorrindo,"* she said, shaking her head. "The smiling fool."

She slid a bowl of nuts toward him on the bar where it stopped a few inches from his beer.

He picked one nut up and studied it. "Back in the States, Brazil nuts like this go for fifteen dollars a pound. And that's only if you can find a good distributor."

She nodded, leaning back against the back bar facing him, her hands again working at the towel on her belt. "You're in the restaurant business?"

"Hoping to be," he said.

"Well, those fell off a tree out back."

He looked up from the nuts in his hand and into her eyes. She was telling him the truth.

"And down here," she said, going on, "we don't call them Brazil nuts."

There was a slight twist of a smile on her full mouth.

"What do you call them?" Beck asked.

"Well," she said, staring into his eyes, "we're in Brazil. So we just call them nuts."

He smiled back. There was no doubt he could come to really like this woman. Too bad he had a job to do, and that she lived and worked in the middle of the worst spot on the entire planet.

In the mirror over the back bar Beck saw the man he was looking for come out of the restroom door, wiping his hands on what looked like clean jeans.

The picture Beck carried actually was a good one, except Travis was younger-looking and skinnier up close.

"So," Mariana asked Beck, not even looking up at Travis, "what brings you to the Amazon, other than the food and drink?"

Beck watched in the mirror behind Mariana as Travis stopped cold in his tracks, staring at Mariana and Beck's back. Clearly the kid knew something wasn't right, but if he thought he could beat Beck to the front door, he had another thought coming.

"I'm looking for a man," Beck said.

"You don't strike me as the type," Mariana said, a slight smile on her face.

"A *specific* man," Beck said, smiling back at her. "His name is Travis Walker."

Mariana didn't even flinch. And she never let her eyes dart to Travis standing on the other side of the room. The woman was good, very good. And in a poker game, she would be deadly.

"He's in his twenties," Beck said, going on as if Travis wasn't standing back there. "Sandy hair, sort of a weasel face."

Beck could tell without even looking directly up in the mirror that Travis was offended by his poke.

"He's wearing jeans, a green shirt, and this bewildered expression."

Beck winked at Mariana, then turned around on his stool to face Travis across the room.

"There's a mirror behind the bar, genius."

Travis glanced past Beck, then shook his head and eased toward the door, clearly thinking of making a break for it.

"You have a choice," Beck said, standing to show Travis who exactly he was facing.

Behind him he heard Mariana move down the bar and away from his back. The woman was good, and knew when to get into something, and when to stay out of the way. Clearly she had decided to stay out of this one.

"A choice," Travis asked, stepping toward Beck instead of the door.

"Option A or Option B," Beck said, indicating each on a finger. "Option A is that the two of us walk out of here nice and easy, take my Jeep to the airstrip, and begin our journey back to Los Angeles, at which point I will deliver you to your father."

Travis stopped a few feet away and stared at Beck.

Beck could tell at the mention of Travis's father that the kid was near panic. Travis's father tended to bring that emotion out in people. Panic and fear.

"Note," Beck said, going on, "Option A has no blood, no broken bones, no problem."

"And Option B?" Travis asked.

"It would be the opposite of Option A," Beck said, shaking his head. "I wouldn't recommend it."

Travis glanced over at Mariana, who was now standing near the end of the bar. Out of the corner of his eye Beck could see her just shrug, as if to say that Travis was in this mess on his own. Smart girl.

"Well," Travis said, glaring at Beck, "what about Option C?"

"There is no Option C," Beck said.

"Oh, really?" Travis asked.

He lunged at Beck like a football player trying to tackle a dummy, his fists swinging wildly. If it hadn't been so sad, Beck would have laughed.

With a quick step sideways, Beck blocked two of Travis's blows with his arms, took the kid, spun him around, and bent him over the bar stool, hard. The kid's breath was forced from his body like someone had sucker-punched him in the gut.

Then, with a quick snap, Beck got out his handcuffs and got them on Travis.

"Like I said, no Option C."

Beck stood Travis up, holding him like a puppet, and smiled at Mariana, who was standing there looking stunned. It was really too bad he wasn't going to have a chance to get to know her better.

He turned Travis toward the door, only to find it now filled with Harvey and Hatcher. Another of Hatcher's henchmen moved into the room and took up positions behind and to the sides of their boss, and the two playing dominoes stood and stepped forward, clearly realizing they were suddenly on duty.

"Mr. Beck," Hatcher said, moving a few more feet into the room.

For a moment the place was deadly silent.

Beck had no idea what Hatcher wanted, but there

was no doubt it wasn't to honor their agreement. This was why he had had Declan get to the plane and have it running. A man like Hatcher, inside his own little kingdom, couldn't be trusted at anything. Beck has seen hundreds like him in Los Angeles, believing their own press. They thought that simply being in their own world made them invincible to any threat. They were often dead wrong.

"Let me introduce you to Option C," Travis said.

Another guard appeared through the rear door, a whip in his hand ready to use.

Hatcher smiled at Beck. "I believe there's been a slight change in the narrative. An unexpected twist, you might say."

"Which is?" Beck asked.

"The kid stays."

"I paid you for the privilege, Mr. Hatcher," Beck said, his voice level and without emotion. "We shook on it."

"Well," Hatcher said, "luckily for me, I had my fingers crossed the whole time."

Hatcher held up his hand showing crossed fingers.

His men around the room laughed as they were supposed to.

Beck said nothing, and didn't let go of his grip on Travis.

Hatcher pointed to one of his men standing beside the door. "Apparently, young Mr. Walker may have stumbled on a trinket of some value, from what I understand was overheard by my friend Roberto."

Travis struggled to get free now and lunge at Roberto, who was smiling and pointing to a place on the balcony over the bar. Clearly Travis had been talking to someone, about something, and Roberto had overheard him. But that made no difference at all to Beck at this point.

"And as he has located it in my jungle," Hatcher went on, the sickly smile on his face, "I am going to need him to lead me to it." Hatcher stared at Beck. "You understand."

Hatcher motioned for his brother to get Travis.

"Let's go, dickhead," Harvey said, stepping forward to take Travis from Beck.

Beck moved Travis around behind him, standing in front of Harvey. He made sure his motions were slow and not rushed.

"I wouldn't," Beck said, smiling at Harvey. "Really."

Harvey stopped, a stunned look on his mean face. "You're serious?"

"Listen," Beck said, talking over Harvey to Hatcher. "I don't want any trouble."

"Then leave now and don't come back," Hatcher said.

"And the ten thousand?" Beck asked.

Hatcher laughed. "Consider it a tax-deductible contribution to your personal health fund."

"Mr. Hatcher," Beck said, shaking his head, "with all due respect, I'm feeling pretty healthy."

"Not for long, asshole," Harvey said. He stepped toward Beck, pulling his gun from his belt.

Beck hated guns so much that anytime anyone even thought of threatening him with one, all he could feel was anger. And these men really didn't want him angry.

But it was too late.

The gun was out.

Before Harvey could even get the gun up into a firing position, Beck slapped it out of his hand and smashed his fist into the ugly man's face, no doubt making it even uglier, from the sounds of the breaking nose.

Harvey stumbled back into his brother and they both went to the floor in the doorway.

Then, with a spinning kick, Beck caught the guard beside Hatcher in the throat, sending him smashing backward into the wall so hard it shook glasses off the counter behind the bar.

With two quick tosses of nearby chairs he knocked both guards who had been playing dominoes off their feet and into a pile before they could even react.

The man with the whip snapped it at Beck, but with a quick motion Beck caught the whip. The sting of it made him even madder as blood stained his coat sleeve from where the tip of the whip had cut him.

Beck stared at the surprised man for a moment, then yanked hard on the long black leather, pulling the guard right into Beck's punch. The guy went down like a sack of flour.

Beck dropped the whip on him, disgusted.

The two guards he had floored with the chairs were scrambling to their feet as he stepped over and laid them out with two quick blows before they could even get their guns from their holsters.

Harvey was still on the ground, his hands cupping his bleeding face. And Hatcher was trying to get to his feet while pulling out his gun. When would people learn to not pull out guns around him?

With a quick step back to the door, Beck yanked Hatcher up into the air and slammed him into the wall so hard Beck knew it knocked the wind out of the man. With a quick twist of the wrist he took Hatcher's gun and tossed it through the side window, smashing the dirty glass outward.

"We're leaving now," Beck said, his face a few inches from Hatcher's face as he held him off the ground and pressed against the wall.

"You're already dead," Hatcher said, his voice raspy as he fought for breath. "You just don't know it yet."

Beck dropped Hatcher onto the floor, then with one last nod at the surprised Mariana, he grabbed Travis, who kicked and fought every step of the way out of the bar.

Manhandling Travis like he was nothing more than a side of beef, Beck tossed the struggling kid into the passenger seat of the Jeep upside down, then got in and fired the Jeep up. Within a few long seconds he had them clear of the small town and headed down the rough dirt road.

Travis finally managed to right himself, even though handcuffed, as Beck hit a large mud hole and bounced both of them off their seats.

"This is Option B?" Travis shouted over the noise of the Jeep and the wind rushing past them. "Are you kidding me?"

"Shut up," Beck said.

"This is suicide!"

Between their position now and the airfield there was at least one guard station they had passed on the way in. Beck needed to get them past that first and foremost. And for that he was going to need something to shield himself against the gun fire.

Ahead he caught sight of an oil drum standing beside the road, its lid half on. He slowed just enough to grab the metal top, swinging it around onto his lap while keeping the Jeep bouncing down the road.

"I suppose that was Option B too, huh?" Travis said, shaking his head at the oil drum lid.

"Get down!" Beck ordered as they spun around a corner and into sight of the checkpoint.

"Jesus Christ!" Travis shouted, ducking as the guards fired at the Jeep.

Beck slouched, holding the oil drum lid up in front of him as he aimed the Jeep right down the road past the guards. Clearly Hatcher had informed them, and didn't much care that Travis was going to be killed along with Beck.

But Beck had no intention of having either one of them killed.

Bullets smashed the front windshield, showering him in glass, as two bullets stung his hand as they hit the oil drum shield in front of his face.

A moment later the Jeep smashed through the wooden blockade the guards had in place, sending wood flying and the two guards scrambling for their lives. Then a moment later more gun fire from behind them as he pushed the Jeep as hard as it would go, moving the oil drum lid around to protect his back and head from any lucky shots.

Beside him Travis peaked up over the seat, looking back down the road at the receding checkpoint.

When they turned a corner, Beck tossed the oil drum lid into the back and Travis climbed back into his seat from the floor. Now the wind whipped at Beck through the destroyed windshield, and the heat seemed even more intense.

"Okay, okay," Travis said, clearly not happy at the fact that the airport was only a short distance ahead. "Can we have a serious conversation for a second, please?"

"No," Beck said, checking in the rearview mirror to make sure there were no speeding vehicles in sight chasing them. Then he slid the Jeep around a corner and raced it up the slope. He wasn't worried about running into any more of Hatcher's men, since he doubted they could get to the airport ahead of him. To the right of the road the jungle and tall trees sloped upward, to the left was a large ravine that seemed to run for miles. The airport had been built on a large, high plateau a mile or so ahead.

"Listen," Travis said, "we are not going to be able to get out of here. This land out there, Hatcher owns it. This road we're on, Hatcher owns it. The air we're breathing, Hatcher owns that, too."

Beck glanced in the mirror again. Nothing. He spun the Jeep through another corner, power-sliding to keep his speed up while he ignored the kid's babbling.

"All right," Travis said, "I'll give you one more chance to reconsider."

Beck just kept his focus on the road ahead.

"Is that your final answer?" Travis asked, leaning sideways against the door so that he was almost facing Beck.

Beck had no idea what the kid was even talking about, and didn't much care.

"Fine," Travis said, shrugging. "I hope you enjoy the fall."

"Fall?" Beck asked. "What fall?"

This time the kid moved quickly, kicking out at the steering wheel, shoving the Jeep hard to the left.

Beck tried to correct, but Travis's foot was caught for an instant in the steering wheel.

And that instant was long enough.

The Jeep smashed through the brush at the edge of the road and a moment later Beck realized they were airborne over a very steep canyon. And only the tops of the trees were below them.

"This fall!" Travis shouted, shoving away from Beck and out of the open Jeep, almost acting as if he could fly.

Beck went the other way, moving to get as far away from the Jeep as he could while still in midair.

The next thing he knew he smashed down through tree branches and brush, hitting hard on a steep, sloping incline.

His forward motion was far too fast and he tumbled end over end, crashing through brush, his speed out of control.

Then, just about when he thought he had tumbled his last roll and would stop, something smashed into his head, hard.

Blackness replaced the spinning and falling.

SEVEN

Travis heard the gentle bubbling of water before he felt the pain in his shoulder. It took him a moment before he remembered where he was, wondering why his bed had become so tilted and uncomfortable, and why the water in the bathroom down the hall was still running.

Only it wasn't the water in the bathroom that was running; it was a stream.

And he wasn't in bed, staring at the brown-stained ceiling. He was in the jungle, with trees and brush and vines over his head.

The memory of his escape attempt jerked him awake and he opened his eyes, instantly sorry he did so. The world was spinning and every part of his body was starting to report that it hurt.

He closed his eyes and tried to take a deep breath. The exercise came out as a groan.

Slowly he opened his eyes again, willing himself to take more deep breaths, even though it hurt somewhere in his ribs.

The spinning slowly eased and he let himself turn to look around.

What was left of the Jeep was upside down in the stream, one wheel still turning slowly. The big guy who had come to take him back to his father didn't look to be in much better shape than the Jeep. He was stretched out on the bank of the stream, his suit ripped and dirty from the fall. He was either dead or still knocked out, Travis couldn't tell.

Dead would be better, but Travis didn't dare wait around to find out. The guy was quicker and stronger than anyone Travis had ever run into, and the way the big guy had taken care of Hatcher and his men made Travis even more afraid of him.

Having the guy succeed in taking him back to Los Angeles would have been as good as signing Travis's death warrant. That's why it had been better to just shove the Jeep over the side of the road into the canyon and hope to live through the crash. At least if he lived now, he had a chance of survival, even in the jungle, even with Hatcher looking for him. In Los Angeles, with his father, he had none.

And at this point, he had a very short life expectancy if Hatcher found him. Hatcher would keep him alive only as long as he believed Travis knew where the treasure was, and not one moment longer.

Travis forced himself to try to stand, taking into account what moved and what hurt. As far as he could tell, nothing was broken or seriously hurt besides a few cracked ribs. And he wasn't bleeding much from any one wound. But the handcuffs twisting his arms behind his back made it impossible to push himself to his feet on the stream bank.

He eased himself into a sitting position and then pushed back over his hands, bringing his feet up and slipping them through his arms. The movement hurt in about a dozen places, but he managed to get his handcuffed hands in front of him so that he could push himself to his feet.

Again the world spun for a moment, then settled.

He managed to stumble the few steps toward the big guy without falling, then went to his knees. The guy was still breathing and didn't look too hurt besides a large bump on his head.

Travis carefully started searching the man's pockets for the keys to the handcuffs.

"Come on, big man," he muttered to himself, "where's the key?"

Two pockets and no luck.

He kept searching, checking to see if the guy was starting to wake up. So far, so good.

"Where's the freakin—"

At that moment he found the key and pulled it quickly from the big guy's side pants pocket.

"Thank you, God," Travis said, sitting back and working to get the key into the lock. "That's it, baby, come on now."

One wrist sprang free and he flexed it, feeling the freedom of his hand. Then, before Travis could even react, the big guy went from being out cold to full movement. He rolled toward Travis and caught him square across the jaw with his fist, sending shooting pains and waves of blackness through Travis's head.

Travis rolled away down the bank, stopping just short of the water. As his vision cleared he looked up to see the big guy standing above him, swaying slightly, but standing. He was breathing hard and clearly hurting.

"I'm not going back," Travis said, feeling his jaw to make sure nothing was broken. The copper taste of blood was in his mouth, but he didn't think he had lost any teeth in the blow. "I can't go back."

"You're going back," the big man said.

Travis pushed himself to his feet and got into his best fighting stance. He'd taken a few classes in self-defense and boxing back in California, but had quit after getting bored. Right now he wished he had stayed for a few more lessons.

"I'm not going back."

The big guy shook his head and then touched the bump above his ear as if sorry he had made the movement. "You're going back. Let's go."

"Big boy," Travis said, putting on his best show, "you're messing with the wrong guy."

Travis had no doubt that this guy could take him easily, but there were still a few more tricks he could try. As this looked like as good as time as any, since the big guy was clearly not close to top form.

Travis looked past the big man and pretended he saw Hatcher and his ugly brother coming up close. He made his eyes widen.

Then he shouted, "No! Don't hurt him!"

The big guy whirled around to face the made-up foe behind him.

In one motion, Travis bent to grab a rock and brought it up against the side of the big man's head.

The contact was hard, knocking the rock loose from Travis's hand. Travis couldn't believe it had worked.

The big guy went to one knee, but just when Travis thought he would fall all the way to his face on the jungle floor, and before Travis could get out of the way, the big guy hit him with an elbow square to the stomach.

Between the pain from the cracked ribs and the sudden impact of the elbow in his stomach, Travis was lucky to only drop to his knees.

The pain sent waves of blackness over him, making him angry at himself for just not taking a rock to this guy's head when he was out the first time.

Beside him the big guy stumbled to his feet, clearly hurting. "Let's go."

This guy was really getting annoying.

"Who do you think you are?" Travis said, his breath finally coming back to him.

The big guy just stood there swaying in the

jungle heat, the stream below them the only sound.

"You come into my town, mess up my bar, smash up my Jeep, eyeball my woman."

Travis smiled as his wild statements caught the big guy's attention.

"Your woman?"

"I'm gonna take you down," Travis said, staggering as he pushed himself back to his feet. The movement sent pain shooting from his cracked ribs and he used that pain to clear some of the fog from his mind.

"You're not taking me anywhere," the big guy said. "Let's go."

Travis knew now was his only chance. "I'm the master of multizone," he said, repeating back the phrase he remembered from his one class. "I'm going to divide you into attack zones."

Now he was starting to sound like a textbook, but he kept going. "I'll attack you simultaneously, confuse your mind."

He had no idea what that meant.

The big guy just shook his head and then winced at the pain. "Enough. You're coming with me."

"It's on," Travis said.

Making high kicking steps, he moved at the big guy. Then, just at the moment he thought the guy was confused enough, he took a wild swing.

He missed, but the handcuffs still attached to his right wrist swung wind and caught the big guy across the cheek.

"Ahh," the guy said, putting a hand to his suddenly bloody cheek. Then he looked directly at Travis, anger in his eyes. "Why you little—"

Before the big guy could finish his sentence, a fist came out of nowhere and knocked Travis hard to the ground, flat on his back and down into the water. The impact knocked the wind from his chest and again sent shooting pain through his ribs and chest.

The guy waded into the water and reached down to take the key from Travis.

He couldn't let the guy take him, cuff him again. He just couldn't.

Travis jammed out his leg as hard as he could and tripped the big guy forward, watching him fall like a giant tree coming down. The splash was amazingly large.

Then on all fours, Travis tried to scramble out of the stream and up the bank, but the big guy grabbed his ankle and dragged him back.

Not wanting to let the big guy get back to his feet, Travis turned and lunged at him. The force of his body sent the two of them rolling like two lovers in a large bed, over and over in the shallow stream water. Rocks jabbed at his back, water choked him, but he kept fighting.

But nothing seemed to work, as finally the big guy shoved him out of the water and up on the bank.

Travis yanked him by the shirt, using the momentum to pull the big guy with him.

They ended up on the stream bank lying side by side.

The pain in Travis's chest made him take small, shallow breaths, and clearly the big guy wasn't in much better shape and was breathing hard as well.

"You had enough?" the big man asked, not moving.

"Alright," Travis said.

At this point he had no choice. He was going to either end up dead back in Los Angeles, or he was going to have to let this guy in on his secret. Half of a fortune was better than nothing at all.

"Okay, look," Travis said, taking a deep, painful breath, "I think we got off on the wrong foot here. So I'm gonna be completely candid with you. Have you heard of the Gato Do Diabo? The Devil's Cat?"

The big guy just lay there, staring upward. Then he said, "You know what? You're gonna stop speaking now."

Travis ignored the command and went right on. His only chance now was to convince this big guy to help him instead of taking him back to the States. "It's a priceless artifact. Forged out of pure gold, with eyes made of the two biggest rubies the world has ever known. It's worth millions."

Just the thought of it had him excited again, pushing some of the pain away.

"I thought you said it was priceless," the big guy said, still lying on his back.

"Okay, you do not want to argue semantics with a Ph.D. candidate."

The big guy looked over at him. "Ph.D.?"

"That's right," Travis said, lying through his teeth. He held up his hands and put his two index fingers about an inch apart. "I am this close to being Dr. Travis Walker."

The big guy shook his head and went back to staring up at the trees and sky overhead. "You dropped out of Stanford after two semesters. Undergrad."

This guy knew a lot more about him than Travis wanted him to know, and seemed a bunch smarter than he looked.

"Okay," Travis said, holding his arms wide apart, "so I'm this close. But this statue, the Gato, it's like the Holy Grail of the Southern Hemisphere."

The guy said nothing, so Travis went on, trying to convince him to help. At least he was listening.

"Every indigenous tribe has some version of a Gato myth. Legend says it can restore prosperity, make dry streams blue, and fallow fields grow tall with crops. If someone were to bring it back—"

Again Travis found himself excited just talking about his find. So excited that he hadn't noticed that the big guy had rolled toward him. Suddenly the man's hand grabbed his wrist and before Travis even had time to move, had spun Travis around and clicked the handcuff back on.

"We got a plane to catch."

The big guy stood, yanking Travis to his feet with one hand on the back of his collar.

Travis's ribs made him want to scream in pain, but all he could think about was getting this big guy to believe him.

"Listen! The Gato is real, and I know where to find it. That's why Hatcher was after me."

The big man stared up the steep embankment that they had somehow survived the fall over, then pointed upstream. "This way."

He yanked Travis hard and shoved him ahead of him.

"And, oh, Travis," the big guy said.

"Yeah?" Travis said, glancing over his shoulder.

"Don't speak."

"You're a very unpleasant individual," Travis said, stumbling forward. "You know that?"

As expected, the big guy said nothing.

EIGHT

Hatcher sat in the passenger seat of the truck, doing his best to keep his temper under control. He had known Beck was going to be trouble the first moment he had seen the big man. And the way Beck had taken out Harvey and the rest of the men was impressive.

And very annoying.

Harvey had needed medical attention to his nose, and one man had a broken arm from where he had tried to pull a gun. It was lucky for all of them that Beck clearly didn't like killing people, or they would all be dead. Of that, Hatcher had no doubts.

Clearly, whoever wanted Travis had powerful connections and knew how to send the right man for the job. But at the moment Hatcher needed Travis more. And Beck was going to die for standing in the way.

It was that simple.

Harvey, his nose bandaged, swerved the truck into a corner of the gravel road heading from the mine to the airport, following the two trackers on motorcycles ahead. He was taking his anger out on the driving, and twice already Hatcher had told his brother to slow down and not push the trackers while they did their job.

Hatcher knew Beck and Travis had been heading for the airport, but they hadn't arrived there. So Beck was trying to get him and the kid out of the jungle in some other fashion, and that would be their fatal mistake. Actually, arriving at the airport would have been a fatal mistake as well, since Hatcher had three guards close enough to get there ahead of Beck. But it seemed somehow Beck had known that.

Ahead, the two trackers on motorcycles stopped as one pointed over the edge of the side of the road.

In this area, the road to the airport went over a ridge line and to the clearing in the jungle beyond. People outside this area, who didn't

know the jungle, for some reason thought everything was flat. Hatcher had thought that as well
before he came here. In reality, the jungle covered
large ravines and fairly tall mountains, only looking moderately flat from the air because of the sea
of green plants that seemed to cover everything.

Harvey jammed on the brakes and slid the big
truck to a stop on the gravel surface. Hatcher
shook his head and stepped out into the swirling
dust as the three trucks behind them also had to
stop fast. His brother never did anything halfway,
both a good trait and an annoyance at times like
this.

Both trackers had gotten off their motorcycles
and were staring at a break in the brush on the
cliffside of the road.

Hatcher moved over beside the two men and
looked down at the broken brush and limbs.
Clearly something had just gone through that
way very recently. The bank was far too steep to
climb down, and from what Hatcher understood
of the canyon below, the drop was a good five
hundred feet from where they stood.

Hatcher glanced at the tracker for confirma-
tion, and the man nodded. The Jeep that Beck
and Travis had been in had gone over the edge

here. The question was if they were in it or not.

Hatcher directed that the trackers should check the area for footprints, then stood beside his brother, waiting.

"You think they're dead?" Harvey asked, his voice deep and nasal-sounding from his broken nose.

"What am I?" Hatcher asked, not looking at his brother. "Psychic?"

"I want to pull out the kid's tongue," Harvey said.

"No," Hatcher said, turning to face his stupid brother. "What you want is to get the Gato."

Harvey nodded, but Hatcher went on, staring into his brother's stupid dark eyes. "If the savages get it, they won't need us anymore. There will be no one to work the mines. Do *you* want to work the mines?"

Hatcher kept his gaze focused on his brother for a moment, then when he was about to answer, he turned to the nearest tracker who approached, shaking his head. From everything they could tell, the two men who had been in the Jeep went over the side.

Hatcher pointed down into the jungle-covered ravine and asked, "How long to get down there?"

"Two hours," the tracker said.

Hatcher glared at him.

"Or less," the man said.

"Okay, listen up," Hatcher said as all dozen or so of the men with him gathered around. "There are two men in that jungle who are trying to steal from me. I feel like an innocent little boy who's lost his first tooth, put it under his favorite pillow, and waited for the Tooth Fairy to come."

Hatcher stared at each man in turn, making sure each was getting the point. Then he went on.

"Only two evil burglars crept through my window." He pointed down into the ravine to make sure everyone understood who the evil burglars were. "They snatched my tooth before the Tooth Fairy got there."

There were a bunch of very puzzled looks around him at that moment.

"Do you understand the concept of the Tooth Fairy?"

They all shifted from one foot to the other, looking at the dirt of the road like it contained gold nuggets.

"Do you?" he demanded.

No one said a word.

"The *Tooth Fairy,* you morons!" Harvey shouted.

"You lose a tooth, you put it under your pillow, and the Tooth Fairy comes in, takes the goddamn thing, and leaves you a goddamned quarter!"

"Brother," Hatcher said, putting his hand on his angry brother and pushing him back a step. Then he looked at the men and pointed down into the ravine. "They've got my tooth and I want it back where the Tooth Fairy can find it and pay me for it, or I'm going to start collecting other people's teeth."

He stared again at each man in turn, then when he got to the lead tracker, he said, "People like you. I'm going to start collecting teeth, understand?"

This time, to a man, they all nodded eagerly.

Hatcher started back for the truck. "Move out, boys," he said. "It's time to bungle in the jungle."

The headache that the kid had given Beck by forcing them off a cliff and then hitting him with a rock didn't seem to be getting any better. In fact, if anything, the intense heat, thick humidity, and millions of bugs were making it much, much worse.

This place was his nightmare. What was left of his jacket and shirt clung to him like a wet rag, and he was constantly slapping at something either crawling up his leg or buzzing around his face.

Travis didn't seem to be bothered by any of it, even though the bugs were around him just as much. Beck couldn't imagine being able to get used to this place, but clearly the kid from California had. And seemed right at home pushing down the trail ahead of him.

Beck still hoped to get to the airport, but he had no doubt that Declan wouldn't be there, or would be under guard by now from Hatcher's men. Still, with a little luck, he could break Declan and his plane free long enough to get them out of this miserable hell. Then he could go back, deliver the kid to his father, and be a free man again.

"So," Travis said, glancing over his shoulder at Beck, "lemme ask you, the whole 'no guns' thing back at the bar? What was up with that?"

Beck ignored the kid and slapped at a bug the size of a quarter that was buzzing his face and neck, sounding louder than any plane he had ever been in.

Travis pushed through some thick brush, then found an easier way under some trees. "I mean you could'a used one, but you didn't. Strip, toss, toss, strip."

"I told you not to speak," Beck said, as his hand made contact with the bug, smashing it away into the bark of a tree. Almost instantly it seemed that three others took its place.

"I know," Travis said, shrugging, "but come on, is that like what, some sort of nouveau Samurai code or something?"

"Let's just say I prefer not to kill people if I can help it."

Travis laughed he pushed through some thick brush, "You know what they say, guns don't kill people—"

Travis let a limb snap back and Beck had to duck to keep from getting caught in the face.

"—people kill people."

Travis had slowed down and Beck gave him a hard shove in the back, sending the kid stumbling ahead.

"So how often do you work out?" Travis asked, gaining his footing and moving on.

Beck again ignored the kid, but there seemed to be nothing that could shut this kid up.

"Every day? Twice a day?"

Beck said nothing and the kid kept rambling.

"Me, I just don't have the patience," Travis said. "Pumping, running, running, pumping. What's it all for, you know?"

He glanced back at Beck.

"I mean, for you it's obviously about beating the shit out of people."

Beck glared at the kid and again shoved him forward.

The kid had the common sense to change topic, but not enough smart to stop talking.

"What about that Zone diet?" Travis asked. "All the honed-and-toned guys are on that protein jar, right?"

Beck so wanted to take a wad of dirt and stuff it down this kid's throat.

"I tried it, but after two weeks, I had so much bacon and overroasted turkey up my ass, I couldn't crap worth shit."

Beck had finally had enough. "Okay, listen!" he said, grabbing the kid and spinning him around so he could talk to his face. "We are *not* friends. You are just a package I have been hired to deliver."

"Sure," Travis said, shrugging, "you're like the UPS guy. Only without the Bermuda shorts."

"That's right," Beck said, glaring at the kid.

"So you don't care what happens to me once

my father takes delivery? Even if he puts a bullet in my head?"

"At this point," Beck said, "I'd load the gun for him."

Travis looked pretend-hurt. "I thought you didn't kill people."

"I said *prefer*. I could make an exception."

Travis stared at Beck for a long moment.

Beck couldn't tell which way the kid was going to go next. Beck was about to push the kid forward and get them headed again toward the airport when Travis shook his head.

"You think I'm joking, but I'm not."

"Your father's not going to kill you," Beck said.

"Not himself," Travis said. "He'd never pull the trigger. No, he'll turn me over to some guy who works for some other guy and look the other way while they dump me in the Pacific."

"Bullshit," Beck said, shaking his head at the idea of Billy killing Travis. "You're his son."

"I'm just the little sperm that could," Travis said. "That's all. The only thing Mr. Billy Walker cares about is what's good for business. And if it's good for business to have his own flesh and blood whacked by some angry business partner, then so be it."

Beck stared at Travis for a long moment, ignoring the bugs and the heat pressing in around him and the headache still thumping at the back of his skull.

"You know it's true," Travis said. "I'm sure he's screwed you over before."

For a half a second Beck actually thought about what Travis was saying, then realized what he was doing.

"I don't make deals with people like you."

"You don't even know me," Travis said, squaring off in front of Beck as if challenging him.

"You're like all the rest," Beck said. "First they try to run, then they try to fight, then they try to negotiate. And when that doesn't work, they do what you're about to do when you realize there's no way out."

Travis stared defiantly into Beck's eyes, not wavering, so Beck went on.

"You're gonna get down on your hands and knees, you're gonna look me in the eye, and you're gonna beg me for a break."

A look of confusion crossed Travis's eyes. Beck knew he had hit a nerve with that.

"Well, I don't give breaks. No breaks."

"You just don't understand the situation,"

Travis said, still standing his ground. Beck had to hand it to this kid, he had nerve. Not many brains, but a lot of nerve.

"Sure I do," Beck said. "You borrowed money from the wrong guy, you shot the wrong guy, you slept with the wrong guy's wife."

Now even more confusion crossed Travis's face. Clearly Beck had again hit pay dirt.

"Who cares?" Beck asked, leaning in real close to Travis. "It was your decision, your mistake."

Travis didn't move, even though Beck was in close.

"Yeah," Travis said, not letting his gaze waver a second, "what was your mistake? Or is terrorizing people just your life's passion?"

Beck held the kid's gaze for a moment, then shoved the kid in the general direction of the airport and got him walking again. No more conversation. He had never, in all his life, seen anyone who could talk like this kid could.

The frightening part was half the time he made an odd sort of sense.

NINE

Beck was starting to get worried. They had been walking for what seemed like hours through the hot, bug-infested jungle, and there was still no sign of the airport.

"We shoulda been at the airfield by now," Beck said, stopping Travis and looking around a small opening in the trees. In this damn place everything started to look the same. And most of the time he couldn't even see the sky because of the trees and brush around them. For all he knew they had been going in circles for the last hour or more.

"We're close," Travis said, shrugging. "Look, I really need to piss."

"Just hold it," Beck said, trying to get any kind of reading on the surrounding hills that he could see through the trees. Normally he was good at knowing exactly where he was at any given moment, but this jungle could confuse the best, and he was confused.

"Come on," Travis said, his voice almost a whine, "don't humiliate me here."

"Alright, alright," Beck said, shaking his head in disgust. "Just hurry up."

"Unzip me," Travis said, facing Beck.

"What?" He wasn't sure he had heard what the kid said.

"How am I supposed to take a leak with my hands cuffed behind my back?"

"Aw, for godsake," Beck said, shaking his head. How much crazier could this entire assignment get?

"What's the big deal?" the kid asked, smiling at Beck.

"Believe me," Beck said, "I'm sure it isn't."

Travis shrugged. "Never had any complaints."

Beck just stared at Travis. There didn't seem to be any other way to get this done. He sure wasn't going to unlock the handcuffs, not after the trouble he had had getting them back on. The cut on his cheek still stung every time a drop of sweat ran down into it, and his head ached where the kid had hit him with the rock.

Beck stepped toward the kid. "Just don't even breathe."

He grabbed the kid's zipper and yanked it down, then stepped back. "There, now get it over with."

The kid seemed to gyrate around like a bad hula dancer, moving a few more feet down the trail, groaning until he finally stopped, panting. "I can't get it out."

"Hey," Beck said, shaking his head. "Don't look at me."

Travis shook his head and started jumping up and down, while at the same time shaking his hips from side to side.

Beck stood there and watched in amazement as the kid went through motions Beck had never seen a human body go through before.

"Goddamn it!" Travis said, everything about him clearly focused on trying to shake his penis from his pants. "I can't get it."

Then he sighed and with one final shake, said, "Ugh, there we go. That's it."

Beck just shook his head as Travis managed to start to relieve himself, facing away into a large green brush.

"Just hurry it up."

"Hey, I'm sorry," Travis said, glancing over his shoulder at Beck. "When you're being dragged to your own funeral, you get a little tense in the wee wee."

Beck shook his head, even more disgusted.

Suddenly Travis glanced to his left. "What was that?"

Beck glanced left and saw nothing.

"Did you hear that?" Travis asked, glancing around to his right, then back to his left.

"What?" Beck demanded.

"That," Travis said, turning around while still peeing.

Beck jumped back, trying to avoid the stream. Suddenly something grabbed his left foot and yanked him hard. Almost instantly he found himself hanging upside down nearly thirty feet in the air, swinging wildly from side to side from a rope hanging from a high tree limb.

The rope bit into his ankle hard, and Beck tried to bend upward and grab the knot to ease the pain, but he couldn't reach it, and just trying seemed to make the pain worse. Finally he just let himself swing for a moment upside down. There had to be a way to get out of the rope, and he would find it.

Below Travis shouted and cheered as if he had just hit a touchdown. He sat down, scooted back over his cuffed hands, and got them in front of him, then quickly zipped up his pants. Then he smiled up at the swinging Beck.

"Welcome to the jungle, tough guy."

"Okay," Beck said, focusing on Travis standing below him as he swung back and forth. "This warrants discussion."

"Save it," Travis said, smiling. "I'm not here to make friends."

The words Beck had said to Travis earlier seemed harsh, considering the circumstances.

"I've got the key to your cuffs," Beck said.

Travis laughed and shook his head. "I don't think so. Those pants have pockets far too loose."

Travis spent a quick moment searching through the brush, then picked up the keys and Beck's notebook, at the same moment Beck realized by patting his pockets that both were gone.

Travis looked up at Beck, laughing. "I can tell you what you've got, pal. You've got problems."

He quickly unlocked the handcuffs and tossed them in one direction and the key in another. Then, just as he was about to toss the notebook as well, he thought better and opened it up.

"What the hell is this? Your diary?"

"Don't touch that," Beck shouted.

Beck watched as Travis flipped open his notebook and then started reading.

"Shrimp and pea risotto with basil and mint?"

He glanced up at Beck, then went back to reading.

"Couscous with grilled summer vegetables, cilantro, and flat-leaf parsley?"

He stopped reading and glanced up at Beck. "What are you, a chef?"

"None of your business," Beck said, again trying to twist his body upward to reach the knot in the rope that held him, and again failing. Hanging upside down was making his headache a thousand times worse, that was for sure.

Travis shook his head, flipping through more pages of the notebook. "The tough guy's a freakin' chef. I don't believe it."

He closed the notebook and stared up at Beck. "Well, you're Wolfgang Stuck right now, aren't ya?"

With a laugh, Travis turned to go.

"See you around, Wolfie-boy."

Suddenly there was a snap and Beck watched as Travis stepped into a second hidden snare. He was yanked off his feet and into the air beside Beck, swinging wildly as he struggled.

"Aw, shit!" Travis said, trying to reach for the rope around his ankle and failing.

"Give me that!" Beck said as Travis swung close. He grabbed the notebook from the kid's hand, then stuffed it into the front pocket of his pants where it wouldn't fall out.

Beck was about to make some comment about Travis being a stuck partner when through the trees came one of the worst noises Beck had ever heard. It sounded like a large cat howling, only louder and far more threatening.

"What the hell is that?" Beck asked.

Travis only shrugged.

Whatever it was, Beck didn't want to be hanging here, upside down, when it showed up.

Using his body like a kid trying to start a swing, he twisted one way, then timing his movement just right, he twisted the other, getting himself swinging slowly, back and forth.

It seemed to take forever, and he was wondering if his ankles were ever going to work again, the pain was so sharp.

It took him three grabs at the rough tree bark, but finally he got himself swinging enough that he got a grip on the tree, pulling himself in close to it, still upside down.

"Great!" Travis shouted behind him. He was also trying to get to the tree trunk on his side by copying what Beck had done. "You did it. Now what?"

"I don't know," Beck said.

He was holding on to a tree, upside down, with his legs pulled upward and away from the tree. First off, he was going to have to push himself up, literally climb the tree upside down, without the help of his legs, until he could get some slack in the rope holding him.

Suddenly there was another growling sound that echoed through the trees, seeming to fill every inch of the air around Beck.

"Shit," Travis said, working even faster and harder to reach the other tree, "they're howler monkeys."

"Monkeys?" Beck asked, wondering why Travis now looked like he was about to panic. "Jesus, I thought it was something dangerous."

Suddenly there was another growling, howling sound and right below them three of the largest, meanest-looking monkeys Beck had ever seen appeared out of the brush. The things had rough fur, nasty-looking snouts, and ugly, sharp teeth. Beck could smell them clear up in the tree. It was a smell he had only run into in back alleys behind bars where the trash hadn't been picked up in a week.

They circled for a moment, then the biggest of the three started up Beck's tree, coming at him faster than Beck would have thought possible.

The other two went up the tree closest to Travis.

Beck almost didn't let go of the rough bark of the tree fast enough to avoid the swipe of the monkey's claws.

The monkey was snarling at him as he swung away, showing him yellow, stained teeth that Beck wanted no part of.

But no matter how much Beck fought to slow his momentum, he swung back at the monkey. The creature swiped at Beck, ripping his shirt and drawing blood along his chest.

The pain radiated along his entire body, covering the pain in his ankle from the rope. He had no doubt that these monkeys could, and would, kill him.

As he swung back at the big monkey again, the beast jumped at him.

Beck, pulling himself upward, caught the monkey square in the jaw with one of his best punches, sending it flipping over and over through the air to the ground below.

The sound of impact was loud enough to echo through the jungle.

The monkey jumped to its feet and stood there, seeming stunned, then looked up at Beck, snarled, and came back up the tree even faster than before.

Not only were these things big and strong, with sharp claws, but they seemed to be almost indestructible.

"Wish you had a gun now, don't you?" Travis shouted.

Without even slowing, the big monkey reached its original point on the tree trunk and then jumped at Beck again, at the same time as the other two jumped at Travis.

Beck missed his punch and the big thing wrapped its entire body around his legs and then started humping him, like a young male dog humping a guest's leg.

"Get offa me!" Beck shouted, punching at the creature.

It ignored him and just kept on working at his

thighs, its hind quarters wrapped around his tied legs.

The other two were doing the same thing to Travis.

"Take him, you animal," Travis shouted, his eyes shut, his hands covering and protecting his face from the two smaller monkeys on his legs. "He's prettier. Look at the ass on him."

Beck had no idea what was going to happen next. He just kept punching at the monkey.

And the monkey kept humping his leg, holding on to the rope and moving away as if the hitting was part of the mating ritual.

Suddenly gunshots echoed through the jungle, very close by.

The monkey on Beck's legs shoved off hard, jumping to the nearby branches of the tree and then disappearing into thicker brush and limbs.

The other two on Travis vanished just as fast.

Below them, from the same direction the monkeys had appeared from, came a large band of men and women. They carried M-16 rifles and wore ragged army fatigues, open over T-shirts. Some had some sort of war paint on their faces.

"Thank god," Travis said. "We're saved."

He and Beck stared at the men below.

Then Travis glanced over at Beck. "We are saved, aren't we?"

Beck had no idea, but at this point anything was better than hanging upside down in a jungle tree being used as a sex toy by a nasty-smelling monkey with long claws and sharp teeth.

TEN

Travis had hoped to never see a rebel camp, but it looked as if that wish had been overlooked in the large wish book. The rebels had cut them out of the trees, then tied their hands behind their back with rope. At this point Travis was sure his shoulders and wrists were never going to be the same after being yanked and held backward so much.

The rebels had then led them for a very long walk through the jungle to what looked like a homeless village under a bridge in Los Angeles. Only there wasn't a bridge, just a clearing of tall Amazon trees and brush.

Around them the jungle had grown dark, with the night sounds of creatures Travis had no intention of ever facing filling the air.

There were a dozen fires going in different places, and the combination of smells was amazing. The odors of roasted chicken and boiling cabbage mixed with sewer smells from a latrine situated obviously far too close to camp. The air was thick, and far too rich for Travis's tastes.

Travis had recognized the one guy in charge as a guy named Manito. He had a reputation of being hotheaded and downright nasty. He was about Travis's age, and looked as if he had lifted weights for years and not showered for months. He clearly wasn't happy as he looked at a wad of money in one hand that he had taken from the big guy. He talked in Portuguese and gestured wildly to his men, often pointing in Travis's direction.

Travis couldn't quite hear all of it, but what he did hear didn't sound good.

And the words "anthill" and "crocodiles" that kept coming up bothered him a great deal. His imagination could only think of bad things concerning those two and his future well-being.

Travis strained at the ropes that tied his hands behind his back. Between the handcuffs and the ropes, Travis knew he was going to be lucky to not have bruises all the way to his elbows. His skin was certainly starting to get rubbed raw.

"Saved, huh?" the big guy said, also straining at the ropes, also without success. "I'm starting to long for a monkey with a hard-on."

At that Travis could only agree.

He fought at the ropes some more, then finally took a deep breath and stopped. "Look, if we're going to die together, at least tell me your name."

The big guy glanced at Travis. Then with a shake of his head he said, "Beck."

"I'd say it was nice meeting you, Beck," Travis said, "but in all honesty, it hasn't been."

At that point Manito turned and headed toward them, waving the money.

The other rebels gathered around, staring at the two of them like they were the main feature after too many trailers.

Travis had no doubt that he and the big guy were about to discover their fate. And from the look on Manito's face, it wasn't going to be good. Travis had to do something, and he had to do it fast, if he was ever going to get a chance to get to his Gato. Or for that matter, even stay alive.

As softly as he could, he whispered to Beck, "Whatever happens, just keep looking him in the eyes and don't blink."

"Won't he take offense?" Beck asked, watching as the group surrounded them.

Of course he would take offense. And that was exactly what Travis was hoping. If Manito focused on the big guy, Travis might be able to talk himself out of this entire problem.

"They're like grizzlies, man," Travis said. "The first sign of weakness . . ."

"Cala Boca, Saco!" Manito and the rebels all shouted at once, the noise echoing through the jungle.

Beside Travis, the big guy held Manito's angry stare.

Travis lowered his gaze and his head, acting as if he were submitting to anything Manito wanted.

"We know you work for Hatcher!" Manito said in Portuguese. "Were you tracking us? What were you doing in the jungle?"

"He thinks we work for Hatcher," Travis said to Beck, who hadn't stopped staring at Manito.

"Well, tell him the truth," the big guy said.

"Honorable host," Travis said in Portuguese, "unlike the man on my right, I do not work for that evil scum. Spare my life and I will lead you to something of great value."

Manito seemed to get even angrier at what

Travis had said, bending over right into the big guy's face and staring at him.

"Why does the giant stare at me?" Manito demanded in Portuguese. "I will cut his eyes out for such arrogance."

"What's he saying?" the big guy asked. "What's he saying?"

"Don't worry," Travis said, "just keep staring at him."

Then in Portuguese, Travis said to Manito, "My friend, the giant is an assassin, paid by Hatcher to hunt down all who oppose him, including me."

As a unit all the rebels brought up their guns and aimed them directly at the big guy.

"Why do I get the feeling," the big guy said through clenched teeth, "that you suck at Portuguese?"

"What did he say?" Manito asked Travis in Portuguese.

"He says he pisses on your ancestors," Travis told Manito. "And dares you to feed him to the piranha before he dies of contempt."

Manito stepped back, so angry that Travis thought the rebel leader might blow a blood vessel in his forehead. He picked a knife from his belt and tossed it to another rebel standing beside the fire.

That man grabbed it, smiling, and started to heat the blade over the fire. Travis didn't like the looks of that at all.

"Cut him loose," Manito ordered, pointing at Beck.

"What's going on?" Beck asked.

"I think he wants to fight you."

"Tell him no," Beck said as a rebel cut him loose and then stepped back. "Tell him I have no quarrel with him."

Travis turned to Manito, who had stripped off his shirt and was doing some sort of stretching exercise that looked like a cross between a native dance and a runner getting ready for a race.

"My friend," Travis said, his voice pleading as much as he could make it while speaking in Portuguese, "the assassin is a great warrior. Much better to shoot him now and get it over with."

Manito ignored Travis and stepped to the fire, taking the handle of the glowing-hot knife. Then he turned and crouched, facing Beck, the knife ready in front of him.

"Look, please," Beck said, holding his hands up in front of him, "I don't want to fight."

Manito ignored him, and his motions, and circled to the right, moving in a crouch, ready to pounce on the big guy at any moment.

Suddenly Manito lunged, thrusting the knife in low and upward.

Beck stepped aside even faster, knocking the thrust to one side and causing Manito to stumble past.

Clearly Beck was going light on the rebel chief, doing his best to not hurt him, as Manito thrust with the knife and Beck blocked or stepped aside easily. The big guy was the best fighter Travis had ever seen.

Finally, after a good minute of going around and around, and Manito having his every move blocked or dodged, two other rebels decided to help out. They stepped toward Beck, both trying to knock the big man down so that Manito could get the knife into his target.

Beck sent one man stumbling away, trying to catch his balance, while at the same time tripping the second and dodging yet another knife attack from Manito.

Another rebel launched himself at Beck.

And another.

The situation was getting desperate, of that

Travis had no doubt. Beck was a great fighter, but even a great fighter can be overtaken by large numbers, and right now Beck was fighting at least five experienced jungle fighters, one with a knife.

But Beck kept his own, moving at a speed that seemed too fast to follow. And as the fight went on Beck started to apply more force to his attackers, knocking one cold into a hut, punching another so hard the guy's nose would never look the same.

And all the while dodging knife thrusts from Manito.

Suddenly, with four rebels attacking Beck head-on, Manito managed to get a knife swipe across Beck's back.

That was like flipping a switch in the big guy. Suddenly he was everywhere, and there wasn't a punch or kick pulled.

The four rebels who had been attacking him from the front suddenly found themselves hurting, or out cold, on the ground.

Beck turned and with a kick so fast that Travis barely saw it from the sidelines, he caught Manito in the throat.

Then, with a quick twist, Beck took the knife

from Manito as he went to his back on the ground, holding his throat.

Two other rebels who had been heading toward Beck a moment before stopped cold when they saw he had the knife.

Beck dropped to the ground beside Manito and raised the knife, clearly intending to kill the rebel leader.

Then Beck, holding Manito down with one hand, looked around at the other rebels, all standing in stunned silence.

Then he looked back into the pained, afraid eyes of Manito and buried the knife into the ground beside his ear.

Then he stood and said clearly, "I am not your enemy."

Travis just shook his head. Man, the big guy was good.

ELEVEN

Beck stood in the jungle clearing, staring down at the rebel leader who had just tried to kill him. Beck's head hurt worse than it had in years, and he ached in a dozen places, besides the stinging cut the rebel had put across his back with his knife.

Beck could see in the rebel's eyes that he had done the right thing in sparing his life, but before he could even offer the man a hand up, two other rebels came in from behind and smashed Beck to the ground.

One hit him across the head with something large and very solid.

Beck fought to keep from blacking out from the blows as suddenly a voice rang through the clearing.

"Pare aqui!"

The two attacking him stopped at once and moved back.

It was a woman's voice, Beck knew that much, and it took his pain-filled head a moment to realize it was the woman from the bar.

"Mariana?" Travis shouted. "What the hell are you doing here?"

"Shhh," Mariana said to Travis, holding up her hand.

Beck somehow, through the pain, managed to push himself to his feet and watch as Mariana strode into the center of where they had been fighting, a rifle cradled in her arm. Clearly this woman was a lot more than a bartender. The way the group of men acted, she was very much in charge.

She faced the man whose life Beck had spared, who had also climbed to his feet, and spoke to him in Portuguese.

The man spoke back, pointing at Beck.

Mariana laughed and shook her head, speaking rapidly.

The guy looked stunned, then said something low, like a kid in trouble, and pointed at Travis.

Mariana glanced at Beck. "You said you would piss on his ancestors?"

Beck turned and glared at Travis.

140

Travis shrugged. "Hey, it's a subtle language."

All Mariana could do was laugh.

Then, from what Beck could tell, she told the rebels that he was a friend, being chased by Hatcher, and within a very short time Mariana was helping tend to the wounded.

Travis and Beck were both fed something Beck couldn't quite put his finger on taste-wise, but it wasn't anything that he would ever serve to anyone in his restaurant. It had a texture of rough oatmeal, and turned to paste when chewed. Still, the paste with three large containers of water was enough for his very empty stomach. Just the water helped ease some of the headache.

As Mariana worked to suture a cut on Manito's arm, Travis stared at her over the fire. Since she had arrived he had been surprisingly quiet. Beck had no doubt that wouldn't last.

And it didn't.

"Barmaid by night," Travis said, staring at Mariana, "rebel leader by day. So all the time I'm working you, you were working me?"

She shrugged and kept on the sutures. "I hoped you might find the Gato."

"And the whole saving yourself until marriage thing?" Travis asked.

141

Beck managed to not snort the bland food through his nose.

Mariana just turned and smiled at Travis. "You're very sweet, Travis."

Beck could tell that Travis had had a monster blow to his ego, and just couldn't let it go.

"I knew," he said, sounding like a little kid. "You know that, right?"

Mariana just kept working.

"All along you know I knew," Travis said, turning back to his food, talking more to himself than her.

Beck finally took pity on the kid and broke in, asking Mariana a question.

"Why?"

He indicated the camp and then the rifle she had carried into camp to make sure she understood his question as what was the need for rebels in the first place.

"Sixty-five cents an hour, Mr. Beck," she said, turning slightly to face him across the fire while still working on the rebel leader's arm. "That's what Hatcher pays the workers. They come from hundreds of miles around, thousands of them, leaving their homes and families. Men like Manito here."

She indicated the rebel leader that Beck had almost killed in the fight.

Manito just ate with one hand while letting Mariana work, never taking his gaze off of Beck, as if Beck was a huge snake and might attack at any moment, no matter what Mariana said.

"But in order to mine," Mariana went on, "you need tools, food, clothing, a place to sleep. You have no money, so what do you do? You borrow from Hatcher."

Beck knew where this was going. It was the oldest trick in history. Governments and bad businesspeople had been pulling it on workers since the beginning of time.

"A pick and a shovel? One dollar a day," Mariana said. "A sack to haul the dirt, another dollar."

Travis sighed. "Mr. Beck knows a lot about debt, don't you? He knows what it's like to dig a hole so deep you can never get out."

Beck stared at the kid without showing a sign of emotion. The statement had come a lot closer to the truth than he ever wanted to admit.

"Call it what you want," Mariana said, disgusted, "it's *escravo*. Slavery, and we intend to stop it."

Mariana finished the last details on Manito's wound, then stood and moved toward Beck, talking as she went. "That's where the Gato comes in."

Travis actually jerked at the mention of the Gato, and again Beck kept from smiling.

Mariana studied the knife cut on Beck's back, pulling his shirt open as she did. Then, without comment, she dipped her fingers in some sort of paste she carried in a small jar and started to dab the paste into the cut.

The mixture felt cold and stung a little. He held still as she worked.

"The herbs in this will keep the cut from getting infected," she said.

"Hey," Travis said, looking up at Beck and Mariana, "wait a second."

They all stared at him, including Manito.

"You wanted me to find the Gato," he said, putting extra power behind the word "wanted."

Mariana said nothing as she finished working on Beck's cut.

Travis went on, clearly excited as his much-damaged ego found something to hold on to. "That means you thought I could find the Gato." He nodded to himself. "Yeah, you really believed in old Travis, didn't you baby doll?"

Beck would have sworn that Travis actually seemed to get bigger just sitting there, as his ego grew back to its normal, immense size.

"We have an expression," Mariana said as she dabbed the last of the paste into Beck's wound and patted his shoulder. *"Homem branco de sorte."*

"Mighty trailblazer?" Travis asked, as she moved back around to sit in a position between Beck and Manito. "Great explorer?"

She smiled at the kid, then stuck the final pin into his ego. "Luckiest white man on the planet."

Travis opened his mouth to respond, but nothing came out.

Manito broke the tension of Beck trying not to laugh at the kid by asking something in Portuguese.

Mariana nodded and turned to Beck. "Manito wants to know who you think would win a fight between Mike Tyson and Muhammad Ali?"

Beck glanced at Manito, surprised by the question. This camp, in this clearing in the middle of the Amazon, just didn't seem to be a likely place to find a boxing fan.

"In their prime?" Beck asked, and Mariana translated quickly.

"Sí, sí," Manito said, nodding.

"Tell him, Ali, hands down," Beck said.

Mariana quickly translated, and then Manito asked another question.

"He wonders about Tyson's power," Mariana said.

Beck smiled. "Tell him he wouldn't have done to Tyson what he did to Foreman in Africa."

Manito brightened at the very mention of Africa, and then in very broken English said, "Rumble! Rumble in the Jungle!"

Beck smiled for the first time since he had left Los Angeles. "Tell him Ali was too smart. He would have used his jab like this."

Beck flicked two jabs out from his body, pretending that each connected by saying, "Bop, bop."

Mariana kept translating to the smiling Manito as Beck went on.

"Ali would have frustrated Tyson, dancing, playing with his mind until—Bam!" Beck threw a hard left uppercut into a pretend body in front of him. "A left to the body."

Then he threw another punch straight away, "A right to the head."

"Float like a butterfly!" Manito shouted, his fist raised, "Sting like a bee!"

Around the camp all the rebels joined in,

146

seeming to know that one phrase in English, almost like a rallying call for their own fight.

"Float like a butterfly, sting like a bee!"

They repeated it over and over as Beck watched, smiling. Then they all started laughing and patting each other on the back. Whatever he had said, Beck knew it was the right thing.

Manito stood and removed a necklace and held it out to Beck. It looked like a gold coin tied on the end of a leather cord.

Then in fast Portuguese, Manito spoke and Mariana translated. "He says you are a great fighter and wants you to have it. It's for luck."

Then, when Beck started to hesitate, she said, "You'll offend him if you refuse."

Beck nodded and took the gift from Manito.

"I'm honored," he said, and Mariana repeated the compliment to Manito.

"Anyway," Mariana said, patting Beck on the arm, "you'll need all the luck you can get."

He glanced at her with a puzzled expression.

"It's a long walk back to the airport," she said. "Especially if you are alone."

Beck shook his head and turned so that he faced Mariana. "I don't think you understand. I'm not going back without him."

He pointed at Travis, who only smiled and shrugged.

"Fifty rifles say you are," Mariana said, smiling at him. The look was both a look of humor and apology. Beck had seen it before, on people who liked him and yet had to do something nasty to him.

Beck glanced around the camp to find that every man had a rifle now pointed right at him. This woman was good. Very good. He hadn't even noticed when she gave the order.

She reached into a pocket and pulled out his money roll and tossed it to him. "And we're rebels, not thieves."

He pocketed the money, and was about to say something to her when a low rumble echoed through the dark jungle around the firelit clearing.

Some of the men pointing rifles at him turned, trying to figure out what the sound was.

Suddenly one of the rebels darted out of the jungle, running as fast as he could while shouting, *"Os gringos!"*

"Hatcher," Mariana said to Beck. Then to her men she shouted a command in Portuguese.

Suddenly a shot cut through the night, louder than the roar from the approaching machines.

The running man who had warned them went down, tumbling head over heels, very much dead from the hole in his back.

Red tracer bullets cut through the night as everyone scattered, firing back into the jungle at the coming lights.

Everyone ducked for cover as Travis sprinted into the nearest edge of the jungle and vanished.

"Travis!" Mariana shouted, heading after him.

Beck stayed a half step behind her, reaching the edge of the foliage just as bullets kicked up the dirt around them.

One glance back told him that Mariana had been right. It was Hatcher and his men, riding in open trucks and Jeeps and motorcycles.

Hatcher stood in the back of a Stinger like Patton inspecting his troops.

Beck, in the camp light, could see that Hatcher was wearing night vision goggles. The rebels didn't stand a chance unless they scattered to the winds.

Then, as Beck ducked under a limb to stay with Mariana, he saw Hatcher point in their direction and shout an order.

"They saw where we went," he shouted to Mariana a moment later as he caught up to her at

149

full run through the dark jungle. "And they have night vision."

Mariana said nothing.

There was barely enough moonlight to illuminate their path. Clearly Mariana knew where Travis would run to in this direction, and wasn't slowing down in her chase of him.

It dawned on Beck that she actually thought Travis knew where this Gato was, otherwise she would have let him go and stayed to fight with her men. But this kid was more important to her and her cause than anything else.

Suddenly she stopped. "He's taking this trail down the hill toward the river," she said.

She then pointed over the edge. "The trail doubles back up ahead. If you could cut down there, you'll come out ahead of him. About a hundred paces straight down. I'll stay on the trail and watch our backs."

The sounds of motorcycles rushing through the jungle behind them convinced him they needed their backs watched.

He nodded. She was treating him like one of her men, and at this point it was just easier to go along. She knew the jungle and wanted the same person he did.

She disappeared into the darkness ahead like a light cloud of mist as he turned off the trail and started down through the brush. He moved as quickly and as silently as he could, which wasn't that silently compared to how he could get around in the city. Here there was always a twig to snap, a branch to hit, vines to catch him. And he didn't let himself think at all about the spiders and other bugs he was running into.

At what he figured was a hundred paces he came across a clear trail as she had said he would. And he could hear someone running at him, not trying to be silent.

Beck stepped behind the trunk of a large tree beside the trail and waited until the person coming was too close to stop. Then Beck stepped out onto the trail and stuck out his arm like a rain road warning sign.

Travis's forward motion took him right into Beck's arm. The kid's upper body stopped, but his lower body kept going, swinging him up in the air around Beck's arm and then down onto the trail hard.

"Not so fast, jungle boy," Beck said, standing over the kid.

Travis clearly had the wind knocked out of him.

At that point the sound of a motorcycle roaring through the jungle grew like a train.

Beck yanked Travis off the ground and tossed him aside just as a motorcycle with one of the native scouts appeared. If Beck hadn't moved Travis, the guy would have killed him.

Then a shot rang through the trees and the man on the motorcycle dove forward off the bike, his limp body tumbling like a sagebrush in a high wind. The bike smashed into the trunk of a tree, trying for a second to climb it before failing and sending the jungle into night silence again.

Mariana appeared out of the darkness, her rifle up and aimed at Hatcher's man to make sure he was dead. Beck had no doubt the guy had been dead before he hit the ground.

"Can he walk?" Mariana asked, pointing at Travis.

Through the trees the sounds of more vehicles coming down the trail echoed through the night.

Beck yanked Travis to his feet, but the kid was clearly still stunned from the hard hit. He grabbed the kid and lifted him over his shoulder like a sack of flour.

"Quick," Mariana said, pointing down and

diving into the jungle off the trail, leaving Beck to follow with Travis as best he could.

Within a minute they were at the edge of the river. Mariana led them to a small boat tied up near a small clearing.

Beck dumped Travis into the boat and climbed in, dropping the old outboard motor into the water.

Mariana untied the boat and pushed them off as she jumped in.

She then reached past Beck and flicked a switch on the engine.

Beck yanked hard two times on the starter cord, then twice more again.

The engine sputtered but wouldn't start.

Mariana said something that sounded to Beck like swearing and then kicked the engine with one foot.

Beck yanked hard on the cord two more quick times, fearing he would flood the old engine before starting it.

Mariana reached over and pulled a knob that looked like an old choke, and with the next pull the engine almost started.

"Mariana!"

The shout rang out from the bank now over thirty feet away.

Manito was running along the trail leading down to the river. The sounds of the engines from Hatcher's group were growing louder by the moment.

"Hurry, Manito!" Mariana shouted. "Hurry!"

Beck yanked on the engine cord again as Mariana pulled her rifle up into firing position.

"Would you—"

"Shut up!" Mariana said.

Beck shoved Travis down into the bottom of the boat and went back to work on starting the engine.

On the bank, instead of jumping into the river to catch them, Manito suddenly swung around and dropped into a crouch, his rifle pointed at the brush behind him.

A moment later three of Hatcher's men appeared from the brush and Manito cut them down with three quick shots.

Finally the engine caught and sputtered to life.

"Manito!" Mariana shouted, waving for him to jump into the water.

"Go!" Manito shouted back as another group of Hatcher's men burst out of the brush along the riverbank. Beck aimed the boat away from the bank and what he guessed was down river as

Manito began firing, taking out as many as he could.

Mariana fired as well, doing her share of damage, but Beck had no doubt that Manito didn't stand a chance. And a moment later he was proven right as a hail of bullets cut the brave rebel down, sending his body flipping over backward from the impacts.

"No!" Mariana shouted, seemingly ready to jump into the river to go back and save her friend. But it was too late for Manito.

Far too late.

Beck grabbed her and pulled her down low as he gunned the engine and sent the boat racing down the river and away from the bank.

Bullets zinged into the dark water around them, and a few pinged off the metal of the boat, but all three kept low in the boat until they were out of range.

Beck could see that Hatcher simply stood in his vehicle and watched, staring at them like an insane child who had had a present taken away.

Beck knew, right at that moment, that this was no longer a simple assignment of getting out a young kid. This had become personal between him and Hatcher, on both sides.

As the gunfire faded, only the engine sounds filled the dark Amazon night, echoing over the still water. The stars and a little moonlight were all Beck had to steer by as he hoped that soon Mariana would lift her head and help him figure out exactly what they were going to do next. But for the moment he and Travis both gave her the time and space to grieve for her friend.

Around them the warm night air seemed to be alive. Beck could not believe where he was, and how things had gone so wrong so quickly. Being in a boat, in the middle of the night, on the Amazon River, with an insane man chasing him, was not his idea of how this mission should have turned out.

TWELVE

After they got a distance away from Hatcher and his men, Beck shut off the small outboard motor on the metal boat and let them drift. There was no point in hurrying too fast in a direction they didn't need to go. The river was slow moving and smooth at this point, and drifting seemed a lot less dangerous than speeding ahead into who-knew-what.

Around them the night was filled with the chattering of animals and the calls of birds. The tall trees were like black walls along the edge of the water, blocking out what little light came from the stars and the moon.

Beck didn't even want to think about what was in the water under them. The city was his place, his environment, not the jungle. And the sooner he got Travis out of here, the happier he was going to be.

Mariana finally raised her head and looked over the water, her hands gripping her rifle as if it was the only answer to her future. Beck could feel the fury radiating off of her. He didn't blame her, considering all the death he had just seen.

Even Travis, who liked to talk, apparently knew that keeping silent at this point was the best for everyone.

Finally, after a good ten minutes of them just drifting through the night, Mariana turned to Travis. With a voice so cold it cut through the humid air like a knife, she said, "Alright, this is the way it's going to be. You're going to take me to the Gato."

Mariana snapped a bullet into the chamber of her rifle with a sound that seemed to echo and re-echo over the calm water.

Beck hated guns, and at this point that sound made him hate them even more. Nothing good was going to come of this.

"And you're going to take me now," Mariana said.

"Easy with that," Beck said, pushing the rifle

aside enough so that it wasn't pointing directly at Travis. "Let's all just calm down."

"Don't!" Mariana said, her fury now directed at Beck. "You saw what they do. Don't ever tell me to calm down."

Beck held her stare for a moment without saying a word. He understood how she felt, but she was going to have to control herself, or none of them were going to get out of this jungle alive.

Without breaking her gaze, she asked Beck, "How many men have you seen die?"

Beck said nothing to the question. It was far more than he was willing to admit to anyone.

"Starve? Suffer? Bleed?" Mariana asked. "What if you could stop it? Look me in the eyes and tell me you don't understand."

Beck understood, all right, but no amount of words were going to help her at this point, so he said nothing.

After a moment Mariana turned back to Travis, again pointing her rifle directly at his chest. "You're going to take me *now.*"

"Or what?" Travis asked, staring at her.

She raised the rifle a slight bit. "Or I'm going to shoot you."

Beck knew that Travis had to be careful,

because with the way Mariana felt, she would shoot him.

"No, you're not," Travis said.

Mariana just stared at him. Beck had to admit, the kid had guts. Not many brains, but a lot of guts.

"Because," Travis said, smiling at her, "if you shoot me, you're never going to find the Gato."

Then Travis did something that not even Beck understood. With Mariana's rifle pointing right at his chest, and her hands shaking from holding in her anger, Travis leaned over and put a finger in the river. Then he licked the finger and paused for a moment, seeming to think about what he had tasted before going on.

"We're close to the Gato, you know," he said. "We're no more than three clicks south of the Verdente Ridge. I can taste the metal in the water. But if you ever want to see the Gato, you're going to have to make a deal."

Now Mariana was just about as mad as she could get without pulling the trigger.

"The Gato," she said, her words cold and slow as she fought to control herself. "It's just an object to you. Life on the Riviera, a private yacht."

"Lady," Travis said, staring right into her angry eyes, "you don't know a thing about me."

"For us, it's hope," Mariana said.

"You're breaking my heart, here," Travis said. "It's a frigging telethon."

With that Beck knew that Travis had pushed Mariana just one inch too far.

"You selfish—"

Beck yanked the rifle up and sideways as it discharged. The gunshot was amazingly loud in the still night air, and echoed over the water for a long time before dying off. Now even the birds and animals were deadly silent.

"Enough," Beck said. He unclipped the magazine from the rifle and dropped it with a thud in the bottom of the metal boat, then snapped the bullet from the chamber, letting it rattle in the boat. The he put the rifle beside him on his seat and faced the two he was forced to deal with.

"He takes you to the Gato," Beck said to Mariana, who looked stunned at the turn of events. "You show me how to get the hell out of this jungle so I can take him home. Deal?"

"Holy shit!" Travis said, still staring at Mariana. "You were actually going to do it. You were gonna shoot me."

With one disgusted look at Travis she turned to Beck and nodded. "Deal."

"Fine," Beck said.

"Bullshit," Travis said.

He stared at the kid. "I could always let her reload her gun."

Travis ignored him and went right on talking. "Let me get this straight. She gets what she needs, you get what you need, and I get the shaft."

"Kid," Beck said, "why do I think that's been pretty much the story of your life?"

"You know," Travis said, turning in disgust to face away from both of them, "I really don't like you."

"You know," Beck said, "I get that a lot."

After thirty minutes of drifting in silence, Travis finally directed Beck to start the boat and take them downstream. Then twenty minutes later Travis pointed to the opposite side of the river at which they had started and told Travis to land.

By the time they got the boat secured and hidden from sight, Mariana decided they should remain in the boat for the short time before the sun started to come up. She didn't know this part of the jungle that well, and walking through it in the dark might be deadly.

Travis had agreed, so they stayed put until the faint Amazon dawn gave them enough light to start out.

Beck felt just about as tired as he had ever felt before. And the idea of going into the jungle again, getting farther and farther away from the airport and any hope of civilization was making him sorry he had made the deal with Mariana.

By noon they had stopped twice for rest, found some fruit for food, and were still moving, with Travis leading the way and Mariana and Beck moving along together.

As they crested the top of a hill, Mariana gave him a long look that Beck caught out of the side of his vision. He turned to her.

"What?"

She kept staring at him and said softly, "Nothing."

"What?" Beck asked again. Clearly she was thinking something, especially with the way she kept staring at him.

She shrugged. "I was just wondering how you came to do . . ." she paused, then went on, "you know, whatever it is you do."

"That's a long story," Beck said.

"It looks like it's going to be a long walk."

Beck stared into her eyes. There was no doubt that if this woman was closer to his home, he would be very interested. Hell, he was interested here, in the damn jungle. So what would it hurt to tell her a little about himself, maybe without all the details?

"I grew up in a rough place," he said. "That's all. One thing led to another. Just like you."

"Like me?" Mariana asked, clearly puzzled.

"You get pushed," he said, "you push back."

She nodded.

"With me," he said, "I pushed so hard the word got around. Pretty soon I was standing in a roomful of the wrong people with the wrong money and no way out except the way I came in."

He stopped and looked at her. "You know what I mean?"

She held his gaze for a long moment, then said, "I like you, Mr. Beck. But you're wrong. I'm not like you at all."

He was about to ask her why she thought that when Travis called from up ahead.

"Coming boys and girls? Or would you like to just stand there and bond?"

Beck broke the gaze and started off after Travis, with Mariana following. This was a conversation that was better left for the moment. He still had a job to do, and considering that Hatcher and his goons were trying to stop him, and that everyone involved knew the jungle better than he did, he had better start paying attention.

A lot more attention.

THIRTEEN

Beck was starting to wonder if he could even walk another step. They had been moving through the thick, humid heat for most of the day, with Travis leading. The kid often stopped and stared at landmarks, sometimes having them backtrack before going on into the jungle in a slightly different direction. If something happened to Mariana or Travis there was no chance that he could find his way back to any kind of civilization. He hated being that dependent on anyone.

Finally, during the hottest part of the late afternoon, they came out of the jungle to find a small waterfall in front of them, cascading over a stone cliff. If Beck hadn't been so tired and hot, he would have admired the beauty of it, and the clear pond that had formed at the base.

The waterfall couldn't have been taller than sixty feet, but just being near it cooled the air like an air conditioner.

Travis kicked off his boots and then dove in, surfacing near the center.

Beck was about to ask how he knew what lived in that water, then decided against it. At this point he was so tired, he didn't care anymore if something ate the kid. At least then Beck could get out of the jungle and go home.

"Take a swim, Wolfgang!" Travis shouted from where he treaded water near the base of the waterfall. "You could use a bath. Just don't pee in the water."

Beck glanced at Mariana and was about to ask what Travis meant by that comment when she smiled and told him.

"A homeless Candiru might follow the stream of uric acid, and swim up your . . ." she paused and looked away from him before continuing. "Well, once it gets in, you can't get it out."

"So what do they do?"

"They have to amputate," Mariana said, smiling up at him and this time holding his gaze, clearly enjoying the fact that the statement had made him very uncomfortable.

Just the thought of the chance of something swimming up his penis was going to keep him out of that water.

Mariana turned to Travis. "Come on, we'd better get going. It'll be dark soon."

Beck glanced at the sky. She was right. They were going to have to spend another night in the jungle without supplies or any kind of bedding or gear. This was, without a comparison, the worst assignment he had ever had.

Travis turned back to Mariana and shouted, "Why? We're already here."

Beck let the words sink in, then glanced at Mariana, who clearly was having the same trouble believing that the long walk was over.

Travis pointed at the waterfall, then shouted, "How cool am I?"

Then a moment later he answered his own dumb question: "So cool. So cool."

It took a minute for Travis to convince Beck that to get to the Gato he was going to have to come into the water. Beck was a strong swimmer, that wasn't the issue. Having a certain body part amputated was.

But when Mariana took off her boots and put her rifle on them, then dove in, he followed.

As they swam toward Travis, the kid smiled, turned to face the waterfall, and did a surface dive.

And didn't come back up.

Beck and Mariana got to where Travis had vanished, and at the same time took deep breaths and dove.

The moment they went down into the water, the sound of the waterfall changed completely. From a soft flowing sound above water to a thumping, low thunder under the water. It was weird, but it almost seemed louder below the surface.

Down about a body length it became clear where Travis had gone. The water under the waterfall was deep, and went back under the rocks a good distance. There had to be a cave back there, not accessible from the ground, only under water.

A perfect hiding place.

Just about the point where Beck was starting to feel he was going to have to turn back to get air, Mariana tapped him and pointed upward for them to surface.

They came up inside the mossy cave behind the waterfall. It was dark, with very little light coming through the falling water.

Travis had pulled himself up on the bank and was standing there as excited as a kid seeing a Christmas tree with a lot of presents beneath it.

"The hieroglyphic code said the great chief of the Marajos put the Gato to sleep behind the 'moving curtain.'"

"A waterfall," Mariana said, holding on to the side of the pool and staring at the water blocking the cave entrance. Then she turned back to Travis, who stood above them on the bank. "But how did you know which one?"

"Try two years, covering a thousand square miles and fifty-three different falls. And add to that I'm a *genius*."

He laughed, the sound echoing through the cave.

Beck could tell that the cave went a lot deeper than it appeared on the surface.

"Yeah," Beck said, still in the water holding on to the bank next to Mariana, "well what are you gonna do for a light, genius?"

Travis pulled a watertight bag from his pocket, unwrapped it, and then pulled out a lighter.

"Option A was a flashlight," he said.

Then he flicked the lighter, turning toward the back of the cave.

The next instant there was a mighty *whoosh* and the entire cave lit up.

Travis was blown backward over Mariana and Beck's head into the water.

Beck ducked under the surface, yanking Mariana down with him.

The intense light of the fire lasted for only a few seconds, then the air above the surface went dark again.

Beck and Mariana surfaced slowly, making sure it was safe.

Beck couldn't believe what he was seeing when he looked around. The walls of the chamber were covered with magical-looking blue flames, all flickering in the slight wind caused by the cascading water at the entrance. The flames lit the entire area, showing them a mouth to a smaller cave at the back of the one they were in. It looked man-made, a lot like a door standing open.

Beck had no doubt it was a very dangerous door.

Mariana said something softly in Portuguese that Beck didn't understand as they looked at the incredible sight of the blue flames.

Travis swam up beside them on the bank, then

felt his face. "Do I have my eyebrows? I still have my eyebrows, don't I?"

"What the hell was that?" Beck asked. Then he remembered all the books and movies about finding old treasures, and how they were all rigged in some fashion. "Was that a booby trap?"

"There must have been some sort of methane buildup," Travis said, pulling himself back up out of the water. "That's all. Five hundred years of it."

Travis glanced back at Beck and Mariana. "Come on, it's safe now."

"Says who?" Beck asked.

"Says me," Travis said.

"Says you?" Beck asked.

Travis shrugged. "I got you this far, didn't I?"

Beck was about to make some comment, but Travis extended a hand to help Mariana out of the water. She glanced at Beck, then took the extended hand.

Beck climbed out on his own, standing with his bare feet on the cool rocks. In fact, considering how hot the late evening was on the other side of that waterfall, and the fact that a wave of fire had just gone through the place, the cave was amazingly cool. It felt wonderful after all the time in the humid, Amazon heat.

But the doorway in the back of the chamber didn't look inviting at all. In fact, it looked like trouble as far as Beck was concerned.

"Follow me," Travis said, turning and moving slowly toward the door in the light from the flickering blue flames dotting the walls.

The door in the wall was a lot farther back than Beck had first thought, and by the time they got close to it, the sound of the waterfall had actually receded some. It was an amazing place, this chamber behind the small waterfall.

"Why do I feel like we're not supposed to be here?" Mariana whispered.

Beck suddenly realized that he was trying to be quiet as well, with the sounds of his own breathing the loudest thing around him.

"Because we're not," Travis said, his voice also low. "The last chieftain of the Marajo people was a man named Igagai Bigi. He hid the Gato to keep his people from being consumed by greed."

Travis glanced back at Mariana. "But the cholera got to them first."

Mariana only nodded as they reached the mouth of the doorlike tunnel. The flames were flickering inside of it as well.

Travis pointed up to the rock over the door. Beck could see a number of skeletonlike faces carved into the stone. There was no doubt they had found something here. The question was, were they going to survive the find.

Travis looked at both of them, then went through the entrance, moving slowly and carefully, looking around with every step.

Beck followed, with Mariana just a step behind.

Inside the opening was a chamber about ten feet high, clearly carved from the stone. It had to be a good twenty paces deep. But just inside the door were thick sticks running from floor to ceiling. There were so many of them that it looked like a forest that they could barely see through to the other side.

But it was on the other side of the forest of sticks that all three of them stared. In the faint light, Beck could see something sitting on a stone alter. It looked like it was a fantastic jeweled skull, staring at them with green eyes lit by the flames on the walls.

If he had to make a wager, it would be that they had found the Gato.

The silence in the room was thick and deep,

so much so that Beck realized he could hear his own heart beating in his ears.

And around them the flames were starting to die out, making it very dark.

"My God," Travis said, softly. "It's there. Over there."

He stared forward, pulling one stick aside as he went.

Above them the rock groaned and dust fell.

It seemed the forest of sticks between them and the Gato had a reason. Like jail cell bars, they were there to keep the Gato in and the rest of the world out, under punishment of death.

And Travis had just walked into that death sentence, as above him the ceiling split open and started to fall.

"Look out!" Beck shouted, yanking Travis back as a large chunk of stone fell from the ceiling, crashing to the floor right where Travis had been standing a second before.

A bright shaft of sunlight burst through from the newly opened hole in the roof as a few smaller rocks followed the larger one, leaving the room filled with dust.

Beck studied the rest of the ceiling as it groaned and seemed to be about to come down.

Those poles had been put there for a reason, and Travis had just sealed their doom if they stayed in this room much longer.

Then Beck saw the one hope they had of actually getting to the Gato. He grabbed the pole Travis still held in his hand and shoved it up under a bulging rock, bracing it against the floor as best he could and then holding on like he was trying to hold up the entire damn world, which it felt like he was.

For the moment his efforts seemed to stop the ceiling from coming down, but he doubted it would last for long.

And he doubted he could hold the pole in position very long either.

"No booby traps, huh?" Beck said.

Mariana looked ahead at the Gato, now clearly illuminated by the light coming in from above. "We can't get through without moving more sticks. The spaces between them are too narrow."

Travis nodded and pointed down at the floor. Even from where Beck was standing holding the pole in position, he could see the pattern on the floor. The entire chamber was tiled. Some tiles were blank, others covered in pictures of a jaguar, others a monkey, and still others a snake. And each animal took a different route through the poles.

"They all lead to the alter," Travis said.

"Three different ways," Mariana said.

Beck strained to hold the pole in place. "How about it, genius? Which way?"

"The path of the cat, man," Travis said. "It's got to be the jaguar."

"That's too obvious," Mariana said, shaking her head. "My money's on the snake."

Before Beck could put his opinion in, which was that they should turn and run before the rest of the ceiling came down on them, Travis stepped forward onto the first jaguar stone.

Nothing happened, so he carefully started to take out the pole that was between him and the next jaguar tile.

"Travis . . ." Mariana said, half turning to run toward the entrance.

Beck got ready to move fast as well.

"One," Travis said, starting to move the stick a little.

"Two." He removed the stick and held it up.

"Three."

No one took a breath. Beck could really hear his heart beating now as they all stared at the ceiling, waiting for more cracks to appear and the ceiling start to fall.

But nothing happened.

"What did I tell you?" Travis asked, smiling and tossing the stick off to one side.

"Don't tell me anything," Beck said as the stick he was holding in place started to slip. "Just do it."

Travis glanced back and up at the ceiling that Beck was managing to hold up, then nodded and stepped forward onto the now open jaguar tile. He took the next pole out and stepped again.

Mariana followed him, staying just one tile behind, taking the loose poles from him and pushing them along the floor and out of the way.

Beck watched, keeping the pole in his hand braced as best he could, as the two of them worked their way through the forest of sticks, getting closer and closer to the Gato.

Then Travis stopped and stared at the floor in front of him. From where Beck stood holding the pole in place, he couldn't tell what was wrong. But there looked to be only one or two poles blocking him from the Gato alter.

"Shit," Travis said softly.

"What?" Mariana asked.

Travis pointed down at the floor.

"What's wrong?" Beck demanded, straining even more to hold the pole in place. "What's goin' on?"

"No more pictures," Mariana said, the sound of worry in her voice very clear.

"Hang in there, Atlas," Travis said. "It's under control."

"Well hurry up," Beck said. "I can't hold this much longer."

Travis studied the path they had cut through the poles, then ahead at the last remaining blockage. Then with a look at Mariana that told Beck he was just guessing, the kid started to pull one pole away, then changed his mind suddenly and yanked another.

All three of them stared at the ceiling, waiting. Nothing.

Travis stepped through the opening to face the Gato.

"Here, kitty-kitty," Travis said, easing his hands around the priceless relic. "Come to papa."

He rubbed the dust off and held it up for Beck and Mariana to see.

Beck had to admit that the huge green opals that formed the eyes were beautiful, and very magical looking, if a person believed in those sorts of things.

Travis held the Gato in front of him. "I did it. I did it. Not the Harvard professors. Not the Oxford archaeologists. *Me.* Travis Walker, son of a pissant gangster and a high-priced whore. And no one can ever take that away from me."

He stared at his prize for a moment, then said, "Ever."

"Travis?" Mariana said, her gaze intent on something on the alter.

Travis didn't respond, but instead just kept staring at his prize.

"Travis!" Mariana said more firmly.

"What?" Travis asked, glancing at her.

"What does that say?"

She pointed at the spot the Gato had been. From where Beck stood holding the roof in place, he could see a slight marking in the stone.

And around them a low, deep rumble was starting to build, as if some angry animal was mad at them.

"It says 'Run!'"

Suddenly a couple of the poles snapped and big hunks of the ceiling collapsed.

Beck held on to the pole in his hand with all

his strength, trying to keep the entrance to the tunnel open.

Mariana and Travis sprinted for the opening, racing along the path they had made through the poles like slalom skiers.

More poles snapped and rocks fell, filling the room with clouds of dust and dirt.

The sound was now so intense, the shaking so hard, Beck could hardly hold on.

"Come on!" he shouted. "Come on!"

Just at the point where he felt the pole was going to explode from his grasp, Travis and Mariana flashed past.

He let go and dove after them, out into the larger cave behind the waterfall.

He hit hard on the rock surface and rolled.

The tunnel belched dust behind him and as he came up running for the waterfall.

Then the ground stopped shaking and it was over.

All three of them stopped and stared back as rocks filled the opening, sealing it forever.

Beck shook his head. They were very lucky that hadn't turned out to be their tomb.

FOURTEEN

Mariana worked slowly and carefully peeling the Konlabos fruit she had found near the pond below the waterfall. She didn't dare take any chance that some of the juice would get in her mouth, or any cut on her hands. This was going to provide a nice dinner for Travis and Beck, after their long day of hiking and finding the Gato. A perfect dinner, as far as she was concerned.

By the time they had gotten out of the cave behind the falls, it had been almost dark. They had decided to set up camp in a clearing a safe distance from the waterfall and scout around for something to eat. That was when she found the fruit. Lucky for her, not so lucky for them, that Travis had never heard of Konlabos fruit.

Now Travis and Beck sat near a fire they had started with Travis's lighter.

Beck picked up the Gato and looked into its eyes, studying it like he would the label on a beer bottle.

"I wouldn't flirt with the Gato's eyes if I were you," she said. "They say it's quite dangerous."

Beck glanced at her, then shook his head. But she noticed that he sat the Gato back on the flat rock where Travis had put it.

"What else do they say?"

"That once restored to its rightful owner," Travis said before she could reply to Beck's question, "the rivers will run deep, laden with fish, valleys green and ripe will bear fruit for centuries."

"And the trees will grow tall," Mariana said, finishing the myth that Travis was repeating, "bringing shade for a thousand hammocks so its people may rest their weary backs."

Beck shook his head, clearly not believing anything about the myth.

"And you think taking the Gato back to your people will do all that?"

She wanted to laugh at him. "No, Mr. Beck. But I expect the money selling it brings will do just that. We can buy seeds, irrigate, farm our own lands, and stay out of Hatcher's mine."

Travis stared at her. "You know that if that statue hits the black market, it'll vanish forever."

"A little late for morals," she said, staring at Travis, "considering you were going to do the same thing."

For a moment she thought Travis was going to stand and come at her. She could see the anger deep down inside, and it was real. Very real.

"Did I ever say I was going to sell it?" Travis demanded. "*You* said I was going to sell it."

Mariana stopped her work on the fruit for a moment and just stared at him.

"You're both such experts on Travis the clown, the hustler," Travis said, his words harsh and biting. "You don't know shit. I was going to put it in a museum."

He shook his head, staring down into the flames of the fire. "My whole life, all I ever wanted, one big score. One shot at the Royal Academy, the Sorbonne. A thing like this goes right, it can undo a world of what's gone wrong before."

He pointed at the Gato. "It was my fresh start."

She had no doubt that he was telling the truth. None at all. For the first time she actually saw him. While she had been working and playing him, he had been playing her after all.

"I'm sorry, Travis," she said, her voice soft.

"Great," he said, shaking his head. "Thanks. A real comfort."

The silence around the fire grew intense as she finished peeling the fruit and handed a part to each man. Finally she had to break the uncomfortable silence, just to make sure they didn't notice what they were eating.

"So, Mr. Beck," she said, "what will you do after you bring him home?"

"I'm opening a café," Beck said.

Now that surprised her.

"Nothing fancy," he said. "You know, ten, fifteen tables."

"Better to be a killer in the kitchen, that it, Mr. Beck?" she asked.

He glanced up at her, startled.

"Such a waste," she said, "your *toca de Midas.*"

"I'm sorry?" he said, clearly not understanding her.

She shrugged and sat down, wiping her hands on her pants to make sure none of the juice from the fruit was left on them. "You ever think maybe fighting isn't the problem?"

Now he looked very confused, but as she went on he took another bite of the fruit, obviously enjoying the taste.

"Maybe the problem is what you are fighting for. *Lutadores da Liberdae,* understand?"

Beck shook his head, then pulled out his notebook and a pencil and started to write. Then he glanced up at her. "How do you spell Konlabos?"

"Oh," Mariana said, standing and moving a few steps away to where she had left her knife. "I wouldn't put them on your menu just yet."

"Why not?" Beck asked.

She took her knife and carefully wiped it off on a large leaf, then again on her pants before putting the blade back on her side.

Travis suddenly seemed to sway and then just tipped over onto the ground with a loud thump.

Beck stared at him, then back at her.

She only shrugged. "Absorption rate is a function of body mass. Still, a toxin's a toxin."

"You're kidding me," Beck said, dropping the fruit in his hand and trying to stand.

He failed and fell over onto his face in the dirt.

She moved to Travis and flipped him over on his back, then dragged him a little closer to the fire. Travis's eyes were staring up at her, panic and anger in them.

Then with a grunt she managed to roll Beck over to a spot on the other side of the fire. He stared at her with intense anger, trying to move and talk, yet doing nothing but grunting and drooling.

"Don't worry," she said, standing above the two men, "after four or five hours, you'll be as good as new."

That got a grunt out of both of them.

She reached down and got the rifle magazine out of Beck's pocket, then clicked it back into place and chambered a shell.

Then she put another few logs and sticks on the fire, making sure it was going strong. "The fire will keep the animals away until sunup."

Another two grunts. A perfect conversation as far as she was concerned.

She picked up the Gato and put it in her pack, then leaned down over Beck. "I know you probably would have kept your word, but money has a way of changing people."

She shrugged. "My people, well, I just couldn't take that risk. I'm sorry."

Beck tried to speak but nothing came out but a low groan.

"Head due north," she said, pointing toward the north so he would know which way it was, " 'til you reach the Quantana Road. Take it south all the way to the airfield."

She moved over and leaned down and kissed Travis on the cheek. "You found it, Travis," she said, staring into his angry eyes. "Just like you said. No one can take that away from you. *Vai con Deus.*"

With that she stood and headed off into the dark jungle, moving slowly and carefully, the Gato in her pack hanging from a strap on her shoulder, her rifle up and ready.

Two hours later, as she worked her way closer to the road she had told Beck about, a distant buzzing sound caught her attention.

She stopped and tried to listen closely. There was something there, a buzzing sound, but she didn't know what it was.

She moved forward a dozen more steps through the thick foliage, coming out into a clearing near the road.

Now the buzzing sounded louder and was turning into more of a chainsaw sound.

Motorcycles!

Hatcher's men. They were almost right on top of her!

She turned and bolted into the thicker foliage, trying to find deep cover to hide from the men on the motorcycles. They were good trackers, but not even great trackers could follow through thick brush and over rock.

Suddenly, as she was running, a branch grabbed the strap on her bag and yanked it from her shoulder.

The Gato rolled out just as a motorcycle burst through the brush coming right at her.

It slid to a stop beside the Gato and then the rider reached down and picked it up.

She was about to take him out with her rifle when another biker roared up behind her, knocking her rifle aside as he went past.

And then another came in from the left.

She eased back into the brush and foliage as three more men arrived, clearly all focused on the Gato instead of her.

Her rifle lay out in the open, too far for her to make a dive for it and kill all of them.

In fact, any move now would just get her killed.

Now that they had the Gato, she didn't matter any more to them unless she did something like try to get it back.

Her stomach twisted as she eased away quietly, sick that Hatcher had the Gato.

But if she and her people had anything to say about it, he wouldn't have it for long.

Three long hours had gone by with Beck unable to move beyond breathing and looking around. He could feel his arms, his legs, his body, but nothing wanted to move when he commanded. Only his eyes seemed to work right, so that he could see the trees over the camp, and the flickering fire to his left.

For most of the last three hours he had watched what seemed like the world's largest spider building a giant web in the branches right over them. More than likely the thing was planning to drop the web on them, and then wrap them and eat them like a taco. Well he wasn't planning on becoming any lunch for any spider.

In fact, the longer he lay there, the angrier he got.

The sun was slowly starting to fill the sky above them with a pink tint, hinting that more heat and another long Amazon day was soon to arrive. Beside them the fire had died down to embers, popping and crackling once in a while.

Just as he had done every few minutes for hours, he tried to move, but his muscles still wouldn't obey his mind's commands.

And all that did was make him even madder.

Suddenly there was a screeching howl that echoed through the jungle around them. It was so loud it startled him, getting adrenaline surging through his system and his heart pumping faster than it had pumped in a long time.

He knew that howl.

Something about the fear must have helped because now he could feel a tingling in parts of his body, like an arm had gone to sleep and the blood was starting to return to it.

He hoped that was a good sign.

With sheer focus of will, he got his head to move upward so he could look around the camp.

There, standing on the other side of the fire, was the giant monkey he had encountered in the trees.

It screeched again, clearly looking at him with much sexual longing.

Shit!

Now the adrenaline was really pumping, clearing out the toxin in his system even faster.

His arms, his legs, his back, were all tingling.

And that made him even angrier.

He pushed himself to his elbows and shouted at the monkey. "That's it!"

The monkey didn't move.

"I've had it! Screw the damn jungle! Gay monkeys, penis-eating minnows, freaky fruit. I hate nature! You hear me?"

The monkey screeched and stepped closer, looking like a lecher about to get a glimpse in the door of a nude bar.

Beck got his legs to move a little, still ranting.

"I want concrete, I want steel, I want glass! I want a nice little organic vegetable garden with Bibb lettuce and earthworms, maybe a honeybee."

He stared at the monkey, daring the thing to come closer.

It did, its eyes glaring at him, its open mouth showing Beck its dirty and very sharp teeth.

"You understand me?" he shouted at the beast. "I want to go home!"

The monkey seemed to laugh at him and step closer.

Beck managed to get to his hands and knees, still facing the monkey.

That was the wrong movement to make it seemed, and the monkey jumped.

Beck caught the creature hard in the throat with a rolling kick, sending the animal running into the brush.

The effort sent Beck back to the ground, breathing hard as the tingling kept getting stronger and stronger.

On the other side of the fire Travis lay there, still unable to move, his eyes wide with fear.

Beck wanted to tell him to not worry, the monkey didn't like skinny kids, but at the moment talking was just too much effort.

FIFTEEN

Even though Travis had objected with language that should not be heard this side of the South Pole, Beck tied the kid's hands behind his back with some vines before they left the camp. The last thing he needed was the kid's finding a way to hit him over the head again.

It took three hours to find the road that Mariana had said would be there, and another eight hours of walking along the road before they got near the airport.

Twice Beck had dragged Travis into the brush to avoid oncoming trucks and motorcycles. And when they finally reached the airport, Beck had tied Travis to a tree and scouted out the entire length of the runway to make sure Hatcher's men weren't waiting for him.

194

They should have been, but they weren't, and that bothered him more than he wanted to admit.

Something was wrong, or something had changed, and until he knew what it was, he was going to move very carefully.

Declan was resting with the dog in the shade of the plane, and the cattle were grazing on the runway. No one else was in sight.

After what Mariana had done to him, and his second close call with the stupid monkey, he was not taking any more chances. When he was convinced the airport, for the moment, was clear, he untied Travis from the tree and walked him out toward the plane.

"Well, whaddya know," Declan said, standing and brushing off his pants as they came out of the edge of the jungle. "Been for a stroll, have ya, lads?"

"Where's my bag?" Beck asked.

"Very nice to see you, too," Declan said, shaking his head.

"My bag," Beck said, pushing Travis to the ground in the shade of the plane where Declan had been sitting. "And some water."

Declan nodded and moved to get them a drink.

"How soon can we take off?" Beck asked.

Declan helped Travis take a long drink from the jug, then tossed it to Beck. "Hang on, now," the short Irishman said. "There's a slight matter of the Jeep you left at the bottom of a mountain."

"I'll take care of it," Beck said, then took a long drink of the lukewarm water.

"In a bloody large puddle," Declan said, still focused on the Jeep. "Am I wrong?"

"I said I'll take care of it."

He stared at the short pilot, making his point very clear.

All Beck wanted to do was get out of this stinking, hot jungle, and right now having Declan go on about the Jeep was the last thing he needed.

Declan started to say something more, but Beck put his hand up for the pilot to stop. "Look, you'll get your money. Now start the plane."

"What's the big hurry?" Declan asked.

"I want to get outta here now, before I run into Hatcher, or any more problems."

Declan laughed. "Don't worry about Hatcher. He don't give a flyin' fornication for you two no more. He's got what he wanted."

Declan shut one panel on the side of the plane and banged on it to make sure it was secure.

Beck glanced at Travis, who was staring up at him with a puzzled expression on his face.

"Whoa," Travis said, before Beck could ask, "what do you mean he's got what he wants?"

Declan shrugged. "They caught up with Mariana in the jungle, snatched up some artifact she was a-carryin'."

"Snatched what?" Travis asked, scrambling to his feet to face the pilot. "What did you say?"

"Artifact," Declan said, right into Travis's face. "Ar-ti-fact. Don't you speak English, man?"

Travis spun around, shaking his head, clearly hurt and mad beyond anything Beck had ever seen in him before. "Aw, Jesus Christ Almighty, Hatcher's got my Gato."

"Your what?" Declan asked.

"The Gato!" Travis said, almost spitting the words into Declan's face. "Don't you speak English?"

Beck pulled Declan back, afraid of what the little man might do next, or what Travis might do, even with his hands tied behind his back.

"Where is she?" Beck asked Declan.

"Mariana?" Declan asked.

Beck nodded.

"Oh, she got away alright. She's pullin' together

the last of her rebels for a little suicide mission, goin' back after the whats-a-ma-gig."

"She's doing what?" Beck asked, almost afraid he had heard Declan right the first time.

Declan shrugged. "I know, I know. *Lutadores da liberdade,* my ass. Freedom fighters."

The little pilot was clearly disgusted at those two words. "More like *lutadores de loco,* ya ask me. They're all gonna die."

Declan turned away and opened up the passenger door to the plane. "Well, all aboard."

Beck stared at the open door. All he had to do was haul Travis up through the door, climb in himself, and survive the flight, and he would be headed home, out of this jungle, out of the fights that went on here.

Yet he knew he couldn't do that and sleep. He knew it deep down inside, and it made him angry. This was how he'd gotten himself in trouble in the first place, this inability to walk away when the walking was good.

He reached into the plane where Declan had put his bag and got out a second pair of handcuffs that he had brought along just in case. Then he turned to the pilot. "How much to watch him while I'm gone?"

He nodded at Travis, who was standing there clearly dumbfounded.

"Say it again?" Declan asked.

"How much to watch him while I'm gone?"

The little pilot glanced at Travis, then shrugged. "Hard to put a price on that."

Beck untied the vines holding Travis's arms behind his back, then put the handcuff on one hand while cuffing him to the door of the plane in such a fashion that the kid could at least sit down and stay in the shade.

"Dude, what are you doing?" Travis asked, staring up into Beck's eyes. "She really got to you, didn't she?"

"We made a deal," Beck said.

"You made a what?" Travis asked.

"I'm at the airfield, but she doesn't have the Gato," Beck said. And now that he knew that he wasn't going to be able to sleep until he held his end of the bargain.

"Are you serious?" Travis asked as Beck finished the handcuffing and stepped back.

"Dead serious," Beck said.

Travis laughed. "Yeah, well, hey, it ought to be a breeze for you."

Beck looked at him. More often than not this

kid had not made sense, and this was one of those times.

"I mean Hatcher's only got a small army back there, with about eighty thousand rounds of ammo," Travis said. "And you know the town so well, too, on account you having lived there for so long."

Now Beck understood that Travis was being sarcastic. He turned away, but the kid kept talking.

"Hey, I got an idea," Travis said, "why don't you saddle up one of these bulls here, ride into town like a Conquistador, and just challenge them all to a duel?"

Travis laughed. "Oh, wait, I forgot, that's right, you don't use guns."

Beck turned from the laughing face of Declan and faced Travis, barely holding his anger in check. "What's your point?"

"You're gonna die."

Beck shook his head and turned back to Declan. He didn't need the kid to tell him there was a chance of that happening.

"The man's got a point," Declan said. "You're gonna die."

"You need help," Travis said.

"And you need the Gato and a chance to escape," Beck said. "That's all you care about."

Travis shrugged. "So, I'm highly motivated. So what? You still need all the help you can get."

With his free hand Travis pointed to Declan. "Hell, you even need him for chrissake."

Declan held up both hands. "Hey, don't look at me! I'm a pacifist."

Beck glanced at Declan, then at Travis, and knew the kid was right. He still didn't have a plan on how to get the Gato back, but he knew that without help, he stood very little chance.

He stepped toward Travis and unlocked the handcuff from the plane while talking. "Travis, I know you're gonna run on me, but I will find you. It may not be tonight, it may not be tomorrow, but I will find you."

He unlocked the cuff on Travis's wrist and stared the kid right in the eye. "And I'm gonna bring you back. You're going back."

Travis smiled at Beck. "Hey, we'll probably be dead in an hour, so knock yourself out."

Beck had little doubt the kid was probably right. But going in there was still the right thing to do. Mariana had been right. It wasn't that he hated fighting, it was just that he had been fighting for the wrong reasons.

Maybe now this was the right reason.

SIXTEEN

The Gato sat like a prize trophy on Hatcher's desk as he stared at the large computer screen in front of him. He hadn't felt this good in years. After all the anger yesterday at that big man escaping with Travis, everything had turned out just fine. Travis and Beck and Mariana had done all the hard work, and he had gotten the prize. He loved the sense of that result, the rightness about it.

After all, this jungle was his.

On the big screen Mariana and a few of the rebels were being marched toward the mine through the jungle. The picture had been taken on one of the many security cameras along the way after the useless attempt of the rebels to rescue the Gato. She and her band hadn't even made it past one of his outposts. Pathetic.

202

Yet there was something about her that attracted him. Something about her willingness to die for everything she believed in that made her very attractive to him.

"Look," Hatcher said to his brother, pointing at the screen in front of him showing Mariana. "See how she comports herself. Look at that posture."

"She's a menace to society," Harvey said.

Clearly Harvey could not see the finer points of the value of human dignity. That was why he would always just be a worker, not much different than those who worked the dirt in the mine.

"Roll it back a little," Hatcher said, glancing at the man sitting at the monitor controlling the tape. "I love this part."

He picked up the Gato and held it, letting the weight of it settle him even more as he watched Mariana on the tape again.

"There!" he said, glancing back at Swensen, who was running the security monitors. "Freeze it, right there."

The image in front of him froze just as he had asked.

"See that?" he said, pointing to the screen. "Her life, her dreams, it has all been ripped to shreds, but still she holds her head up like a queen."

He sighed, wishing he had people like her around him, working for him. He would feel more challenged, less alone.

"That's dignity, Harvey," he said to his brother. "It comes from within."

Harvey stared at the screen for a moment, then nodded. "She's got a nice rack, I'll give her that."

Hatcher glanced at his brother. Why he even attempted to educate the man was beyond him. Harvey was who he was, and there was no amount of training and talking that could change that.

He glanced at Swensen. "Don't erase this. I want a copy for my private file."

Swensen nodded.

Hatcher, with one last look at the Gato in his hand, stood and put it in a wooden case filled with straw that he had had prepared. Then he closed the lid on the box and turned to Harvey. "Take it to São Paulo tomorrow and talk to Gutierrez. And don't take a penny less than twenty million."

"What if I can't get that much?" Harvey asked.

Hatcher shrugged. "Bring it back. It's starting to grow on me."

With that he turned and went out onto the observation deck. Coming up the stairs, led by guards, was Mariana and a couple of the remaining rebels in her little band.

"Brava. Brava," he shouted to his men, applauding their success. "Bellísima!"

Mariana reached the deck and put up a middle finger to him, holding his gaze with intense hatred and anger.

Hatcher loved the way she looked like this, her dignity, her anger and passion.

He stepped toward her. "Man, if I was only ten minutes younger."

He stopped in front of her and looked deeply into her anger. Then he asked the next question. "So, now what?"

She didn't smile or break his gaze. "I was going to ask you the same question."

Suddenly behind him Swensen shouted, "Mr. Hatcher."

Hatcher turned to Swensen, annoyed that he had broken the moment with Mariana.

"We lost contact with Outpost One," Swensen said, his fingers running over the monitoring station, working to get contact back. Hatcher glanced back at Mariana and her anger and beauty, then turned his back on her and went back inside.

"What happened?"

"I don't know," Harvey said, standing over Swensen's shoulder. "It just blinked out."

Suddenly static came from the speaker, followed by a voice that Hatcher didn't want to believe could be possible.

"Mr. Hatcher, are you there?"

Suddenly on the monitor marked Outpost One, a picture appeared, showing Beck's face fully in the frame.

"You got to be kidding me," Hatcher said.

He leaned forward and tapped the comm link to the outpost. "I'm here, Mr. Beck. How can I help you?"

"I have no quarrel with your men," Beck said. "I'd hate to see them get hurt in a process that can be completely painless for everyone."

Hatcher glanced around at his men, then back at the screen as Beck continued.

"For that reason," Beck said, "I'm going to give you two options."

Hatcher tapped the comm link again and spoke. "Sock it to me."

"Option A," Beck said. "You leave the Gato and the girl, voluntarily walk out of town, and never, ever come back."

Hatcher was stunned at the statement, yet said nothing. Around him the monitoring room was deadly silent except for Beck's voice.

"Option B, I make you."

Beck stared into the lens of the surveillance camera, just waiting, as if Hatcher was actually going to take him seriously.

The entire situation was so damn funny, Hatcher couldn't help but break up laughing. A moment later, so did Harvey and the rest of the men in the room, a couple of them almost rolling off their chairs.

Hatcher pushed down the comm link so that Beck could hear the answer for himself.

Beck shook his head. "Wrong choice."

With that he stepped back from the camera long enough to pick up a large stick. Then as Hatcher watched, Beck smashed the security camera, sending the monitor back to static.

The laughter died out around the room as Hatcher took out his pistol and made sure there was a round in the chamber. Then he turned to the room and issued the orders.

"Take the girl and her men down below. Clear out the mine and lock it up."

A moment later a piercing wail filled the air as

the emergency alarms warned all the workers to clear out of the mine and the town. They had all been trained in this drill, and Hatcher could be sure that none of the native miners would be around to join sides.

Then he quickly issued orders for all this men to take up their positions around town. He had a half dozen snipers stationed on various rooftops and mine buildings in the town and along the road to the mine. He would make sure that this Mr. Beck didn't even make it through town, let alone anywhere near the Gato.

The next hour passed quickly as the final preparations were made. Hatcher had no doubt that he was playing it far too carefully for one or two men, yet he had seen firsthand what this Beck could do, so taking no chances was the best way to go.

Hatcher moved to a spot where he could see the main street of the town in the distance from his building. He had a dozen hidden cameras along the main street as well, but seeing something for yourself was always better. And he wanted to see Mr. Beck's death. It would be the final detail added to a perfect day.

The alarms had long been turned off and the

late afternoon heat stifling, not that it bothered Hatcher. The excitement of the moment had him hot enough.

Then, in the distance, Hatcher heard a low rumbling sound. At first he thought it was a distant thunder storm, but the rumbling sustained, and then slowly grew louder.

"What the—"

"Ssshh, my brother," Hatcher said, trying to identify the sound.

"Surveillance monitor at the edge of town has been destroyed," Swensen said.

Hatcher nodded, but didn't turn away from the growing rumbling sound that with every passing second seemed to get louder and louder. It didn't sound machine-made.

So that made it something else.

"The men in town say the ground is shaking," Swensen reported.

Hatcher nodded, now knowing exactly what it was they were facing.

At that moment, in a cloud of dust, a stampeding herd of steer from the airport area thundered into sight.

A dozen of his men broke and tried to run at the sight of the angry cattle coming at them.

Hatcher grabbed a comm link and shouted into it, "Don't run, you idiots! Don't run!"

It seemed none of them were listening to him as the main street of the small town filled with dust and chaos. A number of his men were trampled outright, others were gored by the horns of the creatures and tossed into the air like a child's doll.

When on an open runway, grazing, there didn't seem to be that many cattle, but force them running full speed into the narrow confines of a road between wooden buildings and you get chaos.

A couple of his men tried firing on the bulls, but that just made them angrier, turning half the herd back on those who had survived, while others crashed through open doors, knocked down shade overhangs, even smashed through the front of one building.

And there was still no sign of Beck, or anyone else, for that matter.

More than likely this had been just a diversion of some sort.

Then the gun battle opened up in the streets of the small town, blocked from view by the dust from the cattle, and Hatcher knew this hadn't been a diversion, but a front wave of an assault.

Hatcher smiled. The battle had been joined, and as expected from Mr. Beck, it looked to be a good one.

SEVENTEEN

Travis could not believe how well his crazy idea was working. When he first suggested to Beck that they drive the cattle into town, the man had actually laughed. Travis couldn't believe the big guy could laugh.

But Declan had gone over to his plane, opened a compartment, and pulled out a set of bagpipes.

Declan had guaranteed that he and his dog could get the cattle to town, and then he held up his bagpipes and smiled, saying that the cattle would be damned annoyed when they got there.

Beck had laughed and then agreed, and now here they were, using the dust from the cattle to cover their entrance into town.

Travis tried to see anything ahead of him, but

couldn't. The dust was choking him, and making his eyes hurt, but at least they were at the edge of town and no one had killed them yet.

Travis had picked up two pistols and a lot of extra ammunition from the guards they had overpowered at the outpost where Beck had talked to Hatcher. It had been a while since he had fired a gun, but he figured it wouldn't take long to remember how, especially if his life was depending on it.

Beck, as normal, hadn't taken any guns, just saying he liked it better without.

So Travis considered it his duty to take out the men out of Beck's reach, and let Beck handle the ones close by.

The swirling dust opened enough for Travis to see a guard with a rifle on top of the second building on the right. It took three shots, but Travis got the guy before the guy could even turn and aim at them.

Beck jumped out from directly behind the cattle and onto the sidewalk, making short work of two corporation men who had been stupid enough to come out the door.

Travis cut down another sniper as he leaned forward over the edge of the building, looking for something to shoot at. The guy's fall was right out of an old Western movie, only Travis had no doubt the guy was dead when he bounced off a building overhang and landed on his head on the street.

A moment later a few mad cattle made sure of the point, using the poor guy for soccer practice.

The swirling dust and heat made the fight seem almost like a bad dream to Travis. He would catch a glimpse of someone, fire, and then the target would be lost in the dust again, making it impossible to know if his shot had found a target.

Travis spent a bunch of his time simply trying to stay behind the cattle and in the dust.

Beck, on the other hand, was marching up the sidewalk, taking out one corporation man after another with quick hits or kicks. The guy was a fighting machine, and it seemed the more he fought, the madder and better he got at it.

And from what Travis could tell, right now Beck was damned mad.

At one point two men faced Beck, both with rifles leveled at him, but before Travis could blink some dust out of his eyes, Beck had disarmed both men and they were lying either dead or wishing they were dead in a pile on the side-walk.

Then Beck tossed the guns aside and kept walking.

Finally, in the very center of town, Travis was forced to leave the main dust cloud and jump to cover behind a car as two men with rifles on the bar roof caught sight of him and opened fire.

He shot one man coming up behind Beck, then tried to return fire at the two who had him pinned down, without luck.

Another guard stuck his head out of the bar-bershop door and Travis got him with both pis-tols at the same time, feeling like a gunfighter in the old west.

Only this wasn't a movie, and it was a lot hot-ter and more humid than any place in the west.

Travis ran for an open door just as Beck took out another corporation man by stripping him of his shotgun and then hitting him over the head with it.

If nothing else, Beck had class.

And wow could he fight.

Travis made the shelter of the sidewalk over-hang, but didn't make the door as a huge man with a gun stepped through. With a flying kick, he somehow managed to knock the man's gun from his hands and come up standing.

They stared at each other for a moment, then Travis said, "All right, big man, this is it! You want a little thunder, a little lightning?"

The big guy stared at him the same way Beck had stared at him when Travis had threatened him in the bar. Travis's only hope was that this guy couldn't fight like Beck.

Travis faked to the right, then with a whirling kick that his old instructor would have been proud of, he kicked the man square across the face.

The impact damn near broke Travis's ankle, but the guy went to the wooden sidewalk and stayed there.

Travis stood over him for a moment, stunned. Then he said, "Welcome to the multizone."

Suddenly shots ripped up the sidewalk and the building and the truck beside the sidewalk, sending Travis diving for cover under a nearby old bus.

Very few of the cattle were left between the building to kick up dust, and Travis could see Beck finishing off two guys on the other side of the street.

More shots ripped through the skin of the bus as at least three men on different rooftops were keeping him pinned there.

Other shots rang out above Travis, sending Beck backward to the shelter of a doorway.

Shit. Now they were both pinned down. All it would take would be time until others moved into a position to pick them off.

More shouts pounded into the bus over his head, and a moment later the smell of gas filled the space around him.

Shit, shit, shit, now he had really stepped in it. One spark and he was going to be barbecue Travis.

"Beck!" Travis shouted across the street as a cloud of dust cleared. "Beck, you hear me?"

Beck glanced over his way.

"Let's not stand on ceremony here, alright?" Travis shouted, holding up his gun. "I need some help, goddamn it."

Travis could tell that Beck understood exactly what he meant.

The big man hesitated for just a moment, then nodded. Clearly it had come down to Beck picking up a gun or both of them being killed.

Beck hesitated for just another second, then whatever it was in the big man's past that had made him not like guns seemed to evaporate like so much cool breeze on a hot Amazon afternoon.

Beck dove for a dead company man that Travis had shot earlier, coming up with the man's two guns.

Then, moving at incredible speed across the main road, and with Travis offering what covering fire he could, Beck picked off one corporation man after another that had been pinning them down.

Travis was stunned. The big guy was the best hand-to-hand fighter he had ever seen, but he was even better with guns.

Finally, Travis didn't dare wait any longer as the gas smell seemed to cover everything and shots were pounding into the bus all around him.

With Beck picking off anyone who dared take a shot, Travis scrambled from under the bus. He made it four running steps away before the gas tank on the bus blew up, sending him tumbling.

Too close. Too damned close.

Through it all Beck kept moving up the street toward the end of town and the mine beyond.

He didn't miss a shot.

Travis scrambled to his feet and ran down the sidewalk as one corporation man after corporation man dropped off of roofs or fell through windows.

"Holy shit," Travis said as Beck picked off one guy with the gun in his left hand while reloading the other with his right.

Even though Beck was outnumbered twenty to one, after a few more minutes it just didn't seem to be a fair fight, and some of the corporation men that were left on the edge of town sensed the very same thing and dropped their weapons and ran.

Hatcher and the others in the security room stared at the monitors, watching the mess that Beck and Travis were making of the town. Never had Hatcher seen anyone who could fight like this Beck. And once he had picked up a gun, no one seemed to be able to match him.

But Hatcher knew there were other ways to stop this guy, and since he was headed here, those ways would work just fine.

Hatcher turned to his brother. "Take the Gato and the girl and get to the airfield. You run into any trouble, use her as a hostage."

"What about—"

Harvey pointed at the image of Beck striding

up the middle of the street in town, shooting anything that moved.

Hatcher didn't have time to argue with his brother at this point. "Just do it."

Harvey looked at him, then nodded.

Hatcher then turned to the man running the main monitoring board, the best man with a whip he had ever seen.

"Swensen—" Hatcher said.

But before he could finish his sentence, Swensen finished it for him. "Turn this guy off!"

"Exactly," Hatcher said, smiling at his best man.

Then, as Swensen and Harvey and a few other top whip men headed for the door, Hatcher realized what he had forgotten.

"Oh, and Harvey."

His brother stopped and turned.

"When you're safely out of town, put her out of her misery."

Harvey smiled.

Hatcher knew that sometimes it was a good thing to give his brother a little extra treat.

EIGHTEEN

Beck strode on down the street, a moving killing machine, seemingly angry at anything that moved. He now had a pistol in one hand and a shotgun in the other, firing one while reloading the other.

Travis, scrambled on all fours to get a gun from a dead corporation man lying on one side of the street. He was still shaken from being blown through the air from the bus explosion, and didn't want to think about how many places he was cut, scraped, and burnt. The guns he had been holding had literally been blown out of his hands.

Around him the town was covered in dust and bodies. A few of the cattle were running around, kicking up dust. Not only was the bus on fire, but two of the buildings near it, filling the air with thick black smoke. The crackling from the fire seemed be broken only by the gun battle Beck was fighting.

Travis glanced at the flaming buildings. It would be lucky if this entire town didn't burn down before the day was done.

Travis yanked the .38 from the dead fingers of the company man and checked to make sure it was loaded. Then he looked up just in time to see Harvey driving a 4×4, with Mariana in the backseat flanked by two company guards. The 4×4 cut across the road in front of Beck, heading down a road that circled near the jungle around the edge of the town.

Travis could see a wooden box on the 4×4 front seat beside Harvey, more than likely carrying the Gato.

Beck had been busy with another corporate man that was stupid enough to still want to fight, and didn't see Harvey go past in the 4×4.

"No, no, no!" Travis shouted, running as fast as he could down the road.

He couldn't let them get away. That Gato, and the woman who was tied in the backseat, were his entire life. If they got away now, nothing would be worth living for.

The side road Harvey was taking went along the backs of the buildings and came back into the main road on the airport side of town. There was no way that Travis could get to that intersection in time by running, but he could get there by car.

The old truck belonged to Sam, a guy who cut hair and mostly drank. As with any vehicle in this town, Travis knew exactly where the owners kept their keys, and Sam put his on the sun visor.

Travis jumped into the sweltering heat of the interior, grabbed the keys, and started the old machine up.

Then, before he had even had time to close his door he had his foot on the accelerator, spinning dirt and gravel behind him as he accelerated toward the intersection.

The road Harvey was on was called the West Road, and it came back into the main road right under the town's water tower. It was a blind corner, hidden from sight by a warehouse that Hatcher had built a few years back to house trucks and other equipment.

Travis needed to time this just right, make sure he didn't miss, because there was no way this old truck could keep up with Harvey's 4×4 on the airport road.

He looked down between the remaining few buildings to try to catch sight of Harvey, but no luck. Travis was either ahead of him, which would be good, or behind him, which meant failure. Travis was going to have one chance to stop them, and this was it.

It happened fast.

Harvey, not expecting any traffic on the main road, flashed out from behind the warehouse, spinning the wheel to slide sideways onto the main road.

He didn't even see the coming truck.

Travis timed it perfectly.

The front of the old truck caught the side of the 4×4 right on the driver's door, sending Harvey flying through the air.

The last thing he saw were the wide, beautiful eyes of Mariana as he shoved Harvey's vehicle sideways with the impact.

Both of the vehicles spun and went into the wooden supports of the water tower.

The 4×4 hit something under the tower and flipped, sending the Gato, a number of guns, and one of the guards into the street.

Mariana was tossed clear and Travis smashed his forehead against the truck's old steering wheel.

Finally, after what seemed like an eternity, but was only a few seconds, it was over.

The truck rocked slightly, then settled.

The 4×4 had its wheels, still spinning, in the air.

Both guards looked to be out cold, and Travis couldn't see Mariana or Harvey.

An eerie silence seemed to settle over everything.

Travis pushed himself upright in the truck and tried to get his bearings. There was no doubt he was going to have one hell of a headache from the bump on his head, but at least he was still alive.

A very loud creaking from above the truck was followed by a loud snap as one of the timbers still holding up the huge water tank snapped.

"Aw, shit!" Travis said.

He fought to get the door open as another timber snapped and the huge water tank started down right on top of him.

Beck reached the end of the town and turned toward the mine and Hatcher's observation deck and surveillance room. He hated using guns, but now that Travis had forced him into it, he was going to finish this job with them.

Suddenly a whip snapped out from near a building and wrapped around his wrist, yanking the shotgun free.

With another crack another whip snapped around his neck, sending shooting pains through his body.

Then a third whip wrapped around his other arm, knocking the pistol away.

All three were pulled tight, holding him like a steer getting ready for branding.

Swensen, holding the whip that had his neck laughed. "Any fool can use a gun. What fun is that?"

Beck glanced to his right.

The second whip man had a beard and looked to be twice as old as Swensen's clean-cut look.

The third man looked more like an accountant than a man able to use a bull whip. But Beck could tell in the man's eyes that he would kill without hesitation.

Beck spun his arms loose of the whips, then grabbed the leather of the whip tightening around his throat.

"Well, let's have some fun then."

Beck freed his neck and then yanked Swensen forward and into his grasp.

The other two were fast, faster than Beck had expected, and had the whips snapped painfully back around his ankles. Then, as a team, they yanked hard, trying to pull his feet out from under him.

He stood solid, holding his ground, but they yanked even harder, forcing Beck to use his grip on Swensen to keep him upright.

Swensen swung sideways and back, pulling Beck's upper body forward while the two with whips pulled his legs in the other direction.

Beck hit the dirt hard on his stomach as the two dragged him to the center of the road. Then, before Beck could twist around and untangle the whips from his legs, Swensen's whip came in fast and hard, trapping one arm above the elbow and drawing blood.

Then, with all three pulling as hard as they could, trying to split Beck down the middle, they actually managed to lift him from the ground, then slam him down again.

That hurt, more than Beck wanted to acknowledge.

He twisted as hard as he could, using the full strength of his legs and the weight of his body to yank the two men holding his legs toward him.

They stumbled forward, and before they could catch their balance, he caught the bearded man in the stomach with a sharp kick upward.

The guy dropped his whip and doubled over, fighting for breath.

Then spinning, Beck caught the third man square in the face with a solid kick, sending the man to the road spitting blood and teeth.

Swensen, a knife extended from the handle of his whip, lunged at Beck.

Beck, still tangled in the different whips, swung his leg around and caught Swensen below the knees, sending the man to the dirt, also tangled in the long leather.

Beck quickly twisted the whips around Swensen's ankles.

Then he took another length of the leather, and before Swensen had time to react, wrapped it around the man's neck, pulling it tight to choke the killer.

But Swensen still had the knife extending from his whip handle. With a quick slash, he cut himself free, rolling out of the way as Beck jumped back from Swensen's slashing motion.

But Beck had no plans on letting the man get back to his feet. He ducked inside the knife slash and planted a solid kick to Swensen's chest, sending the man over backward, slamming hard into the dirt of the main road.

The other two were now back on their feet and coming at him, but he used the remnants of the whips still wrapped around his legs to swing out, driving them backward.

Then, as Swensen climbed to his feet, Beck caught him with the whip strap, wrapping it tight around the man's neck.

With a body roll, Beck twisted the whip strap hard, yanking forward and down as he went, using his own body momentum for extra strength.

The sound of Swensen's neck snapping seemed to echo through the buildings, louder than Beck's breathing, louder than the crackling fires.

NINETEEN

Travis slowly raised his head and worked to free himself from where he had ducked to the truck's floor, fearing the water tower would crush him. It had hit the truck, of that there was no doubt, considering the impact he had felt, but only the front and side.

What was left of the tank still towered over the front windshield in front of him.

Beyond the driver's door mud and a puddle of water covered everything he could see.

Travis leaned back, braced himself on the dashboard, and kicked open the truck's door with a loud bang. Twisting around, he managed to crawl out on his hands and knees through the wreckage of what was left of Sam's old truck.

When he hit the mud and water, he made sure he had the .38 in his blood-covered hand. Too many more cuts and bruises and he'd just bleed to death. But at least, so far, he was lucky to still be alive, and if he had his way, he was going to stay that way.

As Travis moved away from the truck on his hands and knees in the mud, he saw Harvey scrambling toward where the Gato lay in the road.

"No way," Travis said softly to himself, then tried to climb to his feet to go after Harvey.

But one of the company guards had a different idea. He seemed to come out of nowhere and pounded Travis back into the truck, knocking him back to his knees in the mud.

Then the guard hit him on the back of the neck, sending Travis flat on his face.

Travis managed to spin over on his back and try to bring his gun up to fire, but the guard was faster. He stood on Travis's gun hand, pinning it, and Travis, into the mud.

Travis looked up at the guy bleeding from a cut across his forehead. He was one of Hatcher's main guards, a guy the workers hated.

The guard smiled down at Travis as he loaded a shotgun.

Travis tried to kick the guy in the back, but all

that did was work to pin him even more, making the guard smile, showing black teeth with one missing.

Maybe, finally, Travis's luck had run out.

The guy aimed the shotgun at Travis and was about to pull the trigger when a shot echoed down the street.

The guy above Travis seemed stunned, then the light in his eyes sort of dimmed, and he toppled forward.

Travis had to move quickly to get out from under the falling body.

He glanced around as another shot rang out, this time the bullet smashing a little part that was left in Sam's truck front window.

Mariana had the second guard by the neck with a wet cloth and was strangling the man, using her still handcuffed hands to twist the cloth tighter and tighter as the guy fired randomly.

The shot that had killed the guy with the shotgun had been an accident. For the moment, Travis's luck was still with him.

Travis watched the final seconds of the fight between Mariana and the guard as she finally killed him, pushing him forward into the mud.

At that moment Harvey grabbed the Gato and

ran for the far side of the street, heading back toward the mine's security compound.

Travis took ten running steps after Harvey, then planted his feet and took aim on Harvey's back with the .38, using both hands to steady himself.

"Nice try, bud," Travis said.

Then he fired three quick shots.

Bullets tore into the building beyond Harvey.

But all three shots had missed.

"Okay, okay okay!" Harvey shouted, covering his head as Travis fired three more shots, again all missing.

Travis shook his head.

How could all six shots have missed? At least he got Harvey to stop so he could hit the guy.

As Harvey turned, Travis pulled the trigger again, this time sure he wouldn't miss.

The click echoed loudly down the street.

"You gotta be kidding me," Travis said, trying to fire again, but only producing more clicks.

Harvey smiled and then turned and ran, slipping as he went in the mud.

Travis had no intention of letting him get away with the Gato. Hatcher's brother was fast, but nowhere near as fast as Travis. Within twenty feet

Travis had caught him and tackled him into the water and mud.

The Gato popped free from Harvey's grasp, sliding like a kid through the mud.

Travis then hit Harvey across the side of the head with the butt of his .38.

But Harvey wasn't finished just yet. With a hard kick, he caught Travis right in the nuts.

A perfect hit.

Perfect power.

For a moment all Travis could see were flashing lights and stars as the pain overwhelmed him. Travis found himself stumbling backward away from Harvey. He dropped the useless .38 in the puddle and used both hands to grab his injured part.

Waves of pain swept over him.

He wanted to just drop to his knees and lie in the mud, but somehow he kept his feet.

A moment later Travis's vision cleared to see Harvey pull a gun from an ankle holster. It was a .38 just like the one Travis had just dropped.

Okay, intense pain was one thing, but dying always had a way of clearing a person's senses.

Harvey pointed the gun at Travis and smiled that sickening smile that Travis had always hated about the man.

"You're empty," Harvey said. "You're so empty."

Travis knew he had a smart remark to make, but he was in too much pain to think of it.

Suddenly, from slightly behind Harvey, Mariana came at full run, diving into Harvey like a football player trying to stop a goal.

Harvey's .38 spun from his grasp and splashed into the water.

Mariana stood over the stunned Harvey, and as Travis watched, unleashed more anger and fury than any woman should be forced to carry.

She pounded on him with her still handcuffed hands, over and over, shouting *"Voce um fiho da puta!"*

Travis had no idea what that meant, and he was convinced he didn't want to.

Mariana kept pounding on Harvey as more of the intense pain from Travis's midsection passed. The Gato was about fifteen feet away, lying in the mud beside two of the steers. Travis started toward it, but the pain sent him to his hands and knees.

Maybe it wasn't past just yet.

He kept crawling, figuring that some day he would get the Gato.

Suddenly, Mariana let out a loud grunt as

Harvey managed to get off a lucky punch and caught her square on the side of the head.

She went down into the mud like a bag of wet laundry.

Shit, Travis thought to himself, forcing himself back to his feet and turning to face Harvey. *Now what am I going to do?*

Harvey stood, swaying as well from the beating that Mariana had given him, staring at Travis.

Just beyond both, the Gato lay on the ground, its green eyes staring at them, waiting.

Hatcher watched on the security monitors as Beck killed Swensen, then kept fighting with the other two company men with whips. All the while he was shaking his head. It seemed that if you wanted something done these days, you had to do it yourself.

He moved over to a safe and opened it, revealing an antique box he kept in there. He loved the feel of the wood and the carvings in the box, but it was what was inside that he really treasured.

He opened the box and took out a pearl-handled pistol. He checked to make sure it was loaded, then hefted it in his hand. The perfect weapon to end all this stupidity.

And the day had started out so well, with the capture of both the Gato and the end of the rebels. Now it was time to end the day just as well with the death of Mr. Beck.

Holding the gun in one hand, he turned and headed out the door.

Beck hadn't had so much trouble with three men in his life. All were experienced fighters, of that there was no doubt. And the two remaining ones were going to try using the long-bladed knife ends of their whip handles, coming at him slashing and hacking at him with deadly force.

Beck stood in the dusty street, poised, the body of Swensen at his feet. It took them a moment to realize that their leader was dead. Beck hoped it might make them turn and run, but instead it made them angry. They both charged him at once, knives out and ready.

He faked to the right and then rolled left, tumbling out of the way of the knife thrusts.

The guy closest, the one with the beard, dove at him, knife held high, so Beck rolled under him and thrust upward with a kick, sending the man flying backward with a loud thud into the dirt.

The other guy, seeing Beck on his back on the

ground, grabbed the remaining leather on his whip and swung the knife end at Beck, like a giant weed cutter, with Beck playing the part of the weed.

Beck managed to roll just out of the way as the knife barely missed.

The bearded guy was climbing back to his feet as Beck ducked another slashing swing of the knife end of the whip.

Then, as a team, the two remaining company men both charged him, coming in hard, knives extended.

The bearded guy came in a fraction of a second ahead of the other guy, so Beck twisted under his knife thrust, kicking the trail whip up and over a hand rail near the sidewalk.

The whip got tangled on the railing just as the second guy attacked.

Beck pivoted, caught the man with a hard punch, then moved to the right in such a fashion that his whip end also got caught on the rail.

It slowed them both down enough that Beck could attack them instead of being on the defensive. He moved in quickly, ducking under one knife thrust and using the man's forward motion to bring him around and thrust the knife into the bearded guy's chest.

Then, with a hard twisting motion, he brought the knife out of the first guy's chest and around and into the neck of the second man.

The look in the guy's eyes was one of surprise, then horror, as Beck let him drop to the dirt holding his own knife sticking out of his neck. After a short moment on his knees, he dropped face down on top of his fellow fighter's body.

Three down, now only Hatcher and his brother to go.

The moment of staring at each other lasted for an eternity between Travis and Harvey. Travis hated the man's looks anyway, but now he was downright ugly, covered in mud and wanting to kill. It wasn't a look that was good on anyone, especially Harvey.

Mariana lay unconscious on the ground. The Gato sat in the mud, watching them with its green eyes.

After the long moment was up, Harvey and Travis moved at each other, kicking and punching.

Travis got the upper hand first, pinning Harvey on the bottom, landing punch after punch into the man's face and stomach.

Then Harvey managed to hit back, knocking

Travis over. Faster than anything Travis had ever seen, Harvey was on top of him, pushing his face under the shallow water and into the mud, holding him there.

He's trying to drown me!

Travis hated the idea of dying, but he hated the idea of drowning in the middle of a street even more.

He fought back, blindly hitting and kicking at the weight and grip holding him down.

No luck. He couldn't budge the guy.

And all the movement was draining the last of his air. He needed air and he needed it now!

He twisted sideways and managed to get a leg up between himself and Harvey before the guy got him back straight.

Using all his panicked might, he kicked upward as hard as he could.

Harvey lost his grip and flew backward, landing on his back.

Both of them scrambled back to their feet, panting and again staring at each other.

Hot Amazon air never tasted so good, as far as Travis was concerned.

Then, as they stood there, staring at each other, panting, Travis realized that Harvey's loaded gun was somewhere at his feet in the water between the two of them.

Harvey, it seemed, realized the same thing.

At the same instant both dove for the puddle, madly feeling around in the mud like they were chasing a fish that they couldn't quite get a grip on, but couldn't let get away.

A moment later Travis found the gun and brought it up, only to see Harvey do the same thing, with the same-looking gun.

Both guns were covered in mud, and both looked like the one Travis had emptied firing at Harvey.

"You're out of bullets," Harvey said, a sneer crossing his mud-encrusted face.

"You're out of bullets," Travis said.

"Uh-uh," Harvey said, "you are."

"You are."

"No, I'm not!"

"Wanna bet?"

Both men stared at each other for a moment, standing there in the mud.

"You first," Harvey said.

"No, you," Travis replied, smiling at the man.

"What's the difference?"

"Then pull."

"Okay," Harvey said.

Travis thought his heart was going to explode right out of his chest as Harvey, at almost point-blank range, pulled the trigger.

Click.

Click.

Travis let out a deep breath, then smiled at the wide-eyed Harvey. "Told you."

Travis pulled the trigger, the gun kicking in his hands as a hole appeared in Harvey's chest and the big man went over backward.

Travis put two more shots into the man before he hit the dirt, just to make sure he hadn't missed this time.

Then he stepped over and picked up the Gato, holding it like a newborn child in his arms before looking around.

Nothing but bodies and a few steers on the main street. Mariana was out cold, and would be for a little longer. The road out of town was clear, and he had the Gato. No one was gonna stop him.

He stared at Mariana, then at the open road, then back at the beautiful woman lying in the mud.

It would be so easy to just turn and leave.

And who would blame him?

TWENTY

Beck stood very still in the middle of the street, his hands away from his sides. One shot from a sniper on the roof of the monitoring building had grazed his shoe, as Hatcher, from the deck, had ordered him to stop, or the next shot would kill him.

Then Hatcher had slowly walked down the stairs, a pearl-handled pistol in his hand, pointing at the ground.

He ended up standing, facing Beck in the middle of the road, looking as if he was in as much control as always, even though most of his men were dead.

Beck had to admit, this guy had an ego that was unmatched, even by the Southern California standards Beck was used to.

Suddenly, from behind Beck a shot cut through the silence of the hot afternoon.

The sniper that had been on the roof grabbed his chest, flipping his rifle out into the air as he went over forward.

Beck glanced back to see Travis smiling from the corner of a building, a pistol aimed at the sniper.

As the sniper fell, his rifle spun outward.

Beck stepped forward and caught it at the same moment the man's body hit the dirt with a loud thud.

Then with a spinning motion, Beck turned the rifle around and aimed it at Hatcher's head.

Hatcher looked at his dead employee for a long moment, seemingly stunned at the change of events, then back at Beck and the rifle pointing at him.

Beck was amazed. The man didn't even seem to blink, or acknowledge that Beck now had the upper hand.

"You are seriously ruining my very fine day, Mr. Beck."

Even though Beck had the rifle aimed directly at Hatcher, the man started to raise the pearl-handled pistol.

Beck lowered his sights and shot Hatcher through the fleshy part of his arm.

The pistol flipped backward and landed in the dirt as the impact spun Hatcher backward a half step.

"Ouch," Hatcher said, holding his bleeding arm for a moment and staring at Beck.

This guy was completely nuts. Beck had no doubt he was going to have to kill him, but it only seemed fair at this point to give the guy one more chance to save himself.

"I'm about to do something," Beck said, the rifle still pointing at Hatcher, "that I've never done before."

"What's that?" Hatcher asked.

"I'm gonna give you a break," Beck said. "I came down here to pick up a man, bring him home. I wanted to get paid, and then move on. That's it. Seems to me eventually there comes a time for all of us, when it's time to move on."

Beck stared at Hatcher, the gun level at the man's chest.

"Mr. Hatcher, it's time for you to move on."

Hatcher smiled at Beck, then took a step toward his pistol in the dirt.

"Wow," Hatcher said, "you *have* reached into the wrong refrigerator."

Hatcher picked up the gun, but before Beck could warn him to drop it, a shot echoed over the dirt road from Beck's left, striking Hatcher in his good arm.

Again Hatcher's gun hit the dirt, sliding another step away.

Beck spun around to see Mariana standing there, her hands cuffed, a pistol held in them.

Hatcher, bleeding now from both arms, stood and faced his two attackers.

There was movement to Beck's left as some of the miners, realizing that the fighting was mostly over, started to come out into the streets.

Behind Mariana, at the edge of town, others stepped from the jungle.

"Wait a minute," Hatcher said, one blood-covered hand holding an injured arm. He stared around him as the miners approached, then back directly at Beck. "Hold your goddamned horses. Can someone please tell me why the history of man has been a constant struggle to destroy his brain?"

Beck had no idea what the man meant. Not a clue. Two flesh wounds and he was raving.

Or more likely, he had been raving for years and years.

"Mr. Hatcher," Beck said, trying to convince the man that now would be a good time to take Beck's offer.

"What?" Hatcher demanded.

"Two choices," Beck said.

"Save it, G.I. Joe," Hatcher said, waving his hand as if dismissing Beck like a servant.

Beck glanced around as more of the miners joined the crowd forming a half circle in front of the man who had enslaved them for so long.

"Option A is still on the table," Beck said. "Walk, Mr. Hatcher. It's time to go."

"Option A doesn't work for me," Hatcher said.

Hatcher again stepped back and reached down for his gun. Beck could not believe how totally insane this man was. There had to be twenty other guns in this crowd.

A shot ripped through the skin of Hatcher's leg, making him stop his reach for the gun and jump backward.

Both Beck and Mariana glanced around. He had no idea where it came from. He hadn't fired it, and neither had Mariana.

Hatcher turned to face Beck and Mariana and the growing crowd around him.

"You think you're gonna change the world?" Hatcher shouted, mostly at Mariana. "Knock yourself out. Or you could be sensible. Down with barbarism. Let's not revert to barbarism. Not good."

Again the man bent over to pick up his gun.

Again another shot grazed him, wounding him but not seriously, just as Beck had done. It seemed that no one in the crowd wanted to be like Hatcher and kill him.

Either that or they were all just like a cat playing with a mouse it had caught, letting it live just long enough to see it suffer.

"C'mon," Hatcher said, now looking directly at Beck. "Put yourself in my shoes. It takes ten hours to produce a single ounce of gold. One ounce."

Hatcher held up a blood-covered finger to make his point.

Beck thought the point was made very well, just not in the way Hatcher meant it to be made.

"Add to that equipment and processing cost, not to mention electric bills."

He stepped forward and reached for his gun yet again.

Another shot ripped through the skin of Hatcher's arm, spinning him around, yet still leaving him standing.

Beck had never seen anything like this. The guy had been grazed with bullets five times, and was still trying to pick up his stupid gun. He was surrounded by a mob of people who wouldn't hesitate to kill him now that all the company men were gone. Clearly Hatcher had lost his mind, either now, or a long, long time ago.

Beck would lay money that the mind had been gone for some time.

"Oh, shit," Hatcher said, holding his new wound and staring out at the mob of people. "What did you have before I came along? You didn't have shoes, that's what."

No one said anything.

Beck glanced at Mariana who seemed to be somehow holding her anger in check, but not by much.

"I gave you work," Hatcher cried out like a preacher trying to convince a crowd. "Opportunity. Coin in your pockets."

Then Hatcher's mood seemed to shift, anger rising to the surface.

"You barefoot little Oompa Loompas didn't have pockets before Hatcher came along. I am the heart in the darkness."

He managed to point his one moveable arm to the North, then kept on ranting.

"I am the compass that points North, toward prosperity and freedom and purpose. Pointing *out* of this hellhole. Pointing to some money, you Oompa Loompa morons."

Hatcher slammed his fist against his chest.

"I gave you life!"

Two more bullets smashed into Hatcher's arms, one fired this time by Mariana. Beck was about to put a bullet through the man's head himself, just to stop him from talking.

The two new shots sent Hatcher stumbling backward, but somehow, after all the damage, he still managed to stay standing.

"Okay, okay," he said, now unable to even raise one bloody arm, "bring me the check."

He looked directly up at Beck. "I'm out of here, Mr. Beck. I'll take Option A."

Then to the mob standing around he said, "My father used to say . . ."

He paused, clearly forgetting what he was about to say. He shook his head. "Oh, hell, he used to say so many things."

He glanced up at Beck again with a smile. "The best thing about a conversation like this is that you never have to have it again."

Beck could not agree more.

With that Hatcher turned and started toward the edge of town, limping along as he went. Beck had very little hope for the man making it to the airport without help, and he didn't know of anyone who might help him, let alone even fly him out of the area. More than likely the man would disappear into the jungle and no one would care.

Beck didn't, that was for sure.

The crowd of miners parted and watched Hatcher leave, saying nothing as he went, his head down, his blood dripping in the dirt and mud, just as so many of the local natives' blood had dripped under his control.

Beck had to admit that sometimes there was a wonderful sense of justice to the world. This was one of those times and he had to admit, it felt good.

Mariana had been right. Fighting for the right cause made all the difference.

After Hatcher reached the edge of the crowd and started toward the road into the jungle, Mariana turned to Beck.

"I know you don't like guns, but thank you, Mr. Beck."

She indicated the town, now free of company control. A number of people had turned to start putting out the fires, and Beck had no doubt that the place would continue, only under vastly different working standards and control.

"We had a deal," Beck said.

"Yes, we did," Mariana said, smiling up at him.

"I'm afraid I didn't completely deliver."

"How's that?" Mariana asked.

"The Gato," Beck said, opening his hands to show that he wasn't carrying the statue. "I promised you the Gato."

"Yeah," Travis said from behind them, "but I'm the guy delivering it."

Beck spun to see a mud-caked Travis, bloody and bruised in a bunch of places, walking toward them down the middle of the street, working his way through the miners. He was holding the Gato in his hands. Beside him was Declan carrying the bagpipes that had so driven the cattle wild.

Beck stared in amazement. He was sure he was going to have to stay here, in this hot, sticky place, and search for Travis. But it seems the kid had other ideas.

Travis walked up to the two of them and then handed Mariana the Gato.

"Don't take less than 15.6 million," Travis said. "Not a penny less. We clear?"

Mariana stared at the statue for a moment, then looked up at Travis with tears in her eyes. "I'm impressed," she said, her voice barely stopping from cracking with emotion. "I really am."

"Just make sure they spell my name right," Travis said, smiling.

Mariana nodded and then turned to the crowd and held up the Gato like it was a Stanley Cup.

The miners all cheered and danced and patted each other on the back.

Beck glanced at Travis, who looked happy under all the mud.

When Travis noticed Beck staring at him, he said, "Like I told you, it wasn't just about the money."

They stared at each for a moment, Travis smiling, Beck clearly stunned. Beck had never been so impressed with an action in his entire life.

Again Mariana was right, it wasn't the fighting that mattered, it was what you were fighting for.

Travis had clearly been fighting for the right thing all this time. It was just that no one gave him a chance to show them until now.

"It's your move, big man," Travis said over the cheering and shouting and celebrating that was going on around them.

Beck glanced over at Declan, then back at Travis, then at Declan again, and a plan formed in his mind. A plan that might get him killed, but it would be worth the fight.

"Declan," Beck said, "start the plane."

"Start the plane?" Travis asked, frowning. "What does that mean, start the plane?"

Beck just smiled and patted the kid on the shoulder. "Trust me."

Even with all the noise and celebration going on around them, Beck heard Travis snort at that comment.

TWENTY-ONE

The trip back didn't seem to take as long as the flights into the jungle. For the long leg of the flight Beck had bought him and Travis first-class tickets. Also, they were both so tired, they slept most of the way anyway.

Back in Los Angeles, Beck had taken them to his apartment, where they both got cleaned up again. While he had been gone, Beck's suit had been returned from the cleaners with no sign of the Jägermeister or the blood left on it.

His plan was simple, and had almost no chance of working, but at least it was a plan, a fight for the right side of things for a change.

They were within a half block of Travis's father's house when the kid asked for the hundredth time about the plan, and why shouldn't he be a part of it. After all, it was his life on the line.

Beck had said what he had said from that moment in the street in the jungle. "Trust me. For the moment I have to handcuff your hands again," Beck said, handing Travis the cuffs from his pocket.

"You're kidding!" Travis said. "My wrists are still sore from being dragged through the jungle tied up with those damn vines."

"Just do it," Beck said. "In front this time."

Travis glanced at him, then shook his head and snapped the handcuff on one wrist as Beck pulled in Billy's driveway.

Beck helped with the other wrist before getting out of the car and moving around to open Travis's door. He reached into the backseat and picked up a bag with a special gift in it for Billy.

"Let's go," Beck said, opening the door.

Travis just shook his head and climbed out.

They stood there for a moment staring at the large mansion Travis's father owned. Clearly this was the last place on the planet Travis wanted to be. Or ever expected to be again.

Beck wasn't real pleased with being here either,

but he had to follow through on his promise and give his plan a try.

"Well, waddya know?" one of Billy's guards said, stepping off the front porch.

He motioned that they come forward, then turned and went into the house calling out, "Billy! Guess who's here?"

"Come on," Beck said, pushing Travis forward toward the front door.

Travis glanced at Beck, then at what he was carrying. "What's in the bag, cookies?"

Beck didn't answer the kid as they went through the front door and into the house, turning toward the kitchen.

"Jesus H. Christ," Billy said, coming out of the kitchen wiping his hands on a towel.

"Hello, Pop," Travis said.

"You look thin," Billy said to his son, stopping and looking at the kid.

"Running is good exercise," Travis said.

Billy smiled, then stepped forward and slapped Travis across the face. "You know the shit you caused me?"

Travis said nothing as Billy went on.

"There's not enough aspirin in the universe for a headache like you."

Travis shrugged. "Well, there probably is, but I understand what you mean."

"You do?" Billy slammed Travis down on a stool. To Beck's surprise, Travis didn't wince in pain. "Good. Then you'll understand why I'm sending you back to Chicago to explain your behavior to my very good friend Johnny Strodell."

Travis leaned away from Billy. "Actually, I'm not sure I do understand that."

"Okay, smartass."

"Well," Travis said, "I'm not that smart, Dad. I didn't know—"

Billy's hand caught Travis on the side of the face. This time, Travis winced.

"Don't—"

"—that she was married." Travis's voice.

"She was married," Billy said. "*Very* married." Then he turned to Beck.

Beck didn't wince. Instead, he took the fruit he had brought with him from the bag. Travis obviously recognized the fruit at once, but after a quick second managed to put a poker face back on.

Beck cut some pieces. The goons grabbed some, then Travis reached for one, keeping up the game, but Billy slapped Travis's hand away.

Instead, Billy took one. He bit into it, frowned a little at the taste, and kept eating.

"And you," he said to Beck in a tone that let Beck know that Billy wasn't planning to forgive him.

Beck shrugged. "I did walk him through that door."

Billy started swaying. His eyes were growing red. "What's happening?"

Beck smiled slowly. "Technically, we're good."

One of the goons fell to the deck with a thud.

"Boy, you got a funny face," Billy said, tilting his head sideways. Then he looked at Travis.

Travis moved his hands away from the fruit. "You know, Dad, you're a very unpleasant individual—"

Billy blinked, clearly fighting the effects of the Konlabos fruit. Beck had to work hard to suppress a grin.

"—and a very bad parental figure, but that's pretty obvious—"

The second goon fell, landing with a louder thud than the first. Billy slipped, but managed to hold himself up with two fingers.

Travis leaned down and pried his father's fingers off the counter.

"And," Travis added, "you were always mean to my mom."

Billy hit the floor. He looked up at Beck first, pleading. Beck shrugged. Then Billy looked at Travis. Travis didn't move.

"It's going to be about four hours, Billy," Beck said.

"Yeah," Travis said, "four hours, Daddy. But you're not going to be lonely. I brought you a little something, too."

He got the large case from the back of Beck's truck and slammed it onto the kitchen floor. The case had airholes, warning stickers, and steel bolt latches. Beck's back stiffened. He didn't like thinking about what was inside the case.

Billy stared. He obviously didn't understand. But he would, in just a few minutes.

"When you get over all this," Travis said, "it's going to be a little hard for you. I'm not going to lie. But you will. I'll give you a call. Maybe we can go fishing or something."

Billy groaned.

"Bye-bye, Dad," Travis said.

Then he touched Beck's arm lightly, and they both left. As they walked to the truck, Beck couldn't help looking over his shoulder.

The metal door on the case had opened just a little. A howler monkey peered out. Its gaze found the fallen Billy.

Beck shuddered. He couldn't help it. Then he turned away.

"I thought you had character," Travis was saying, "but I wasn't sure."

"Stop talking," Beck growled.

"But you do, man. You got it! You *really* got it!"

Beck suppressed a sigh. "Get in the car."

"You know, you violated pretty much every agricultural law back there—"

"That's the least of our problems," Beck said. He could not believe what he had just done. No chance of a restaurant in this town, maybe not anywhere, until one of Billy's enemies took care of Billy.

And maybe, without Travis to clear up the mess, Billy might not be long for this plane of existence. Beck could only hope.

"I know," Travis said. "Why don't you just go back in there and finish them off?"

Beck gave him a level look. "You want to go back in there, be my guest. I'll wait right here."

At that moment, a monkey howl echoed from deep inside the house.

Travis swallowed. Hard. "No," he said. "I'm good."

Beck pushed Travis toward the truck. "Just get in the car before I change my mind."

Travis glared at him. "Don't push me."

"Get in the car," Beck said again.

Travis's hand clenched into fists. "I'm serious, Beck. I appreciate what you did back there. I really do. But if you want to get technical about it, all that really did was even up the score, since I saved your life first."

Beck's eyes narrowed. "You did *what?*"

"You don't have to thank me, but if we're going to be free men here, there's not going to be any more of you pushing me around like a little dog."

But, Beck wanted to say, in some ways you are a little dog. Instead, he said, "I'm going to give you one more chance to get in the car."

"*I'm* going to give *you* one more chance to apologize, and it better be a very sincere apology or I'm going to whoop your ass right here. And I'm not going to need any fruit to do it."

Travis started to get that look in his eyes.

This time Beck swallowed. Hard. "Don't do it—"

"It's on." Travis slowly raised his left foot. "Looks like it's about to rain, big boy."

Travis wiggled his foot. Then he grinned.

Beck didn't like the grin.

"I think I hear some thunder," Travis said.

"Travis," Beck warned.

Travis raised his eyebrows, pretending innocence. "Do you hear thunder?"

And then he attacked—knees pumping, seal-barking, fists clenched, closing in on Beck.

Beck clenched his own massive fist.

There was going to be a mighty collision—

And not even Beck was sure who would win.

Visit
❖ Pocket Books ❖
online at

....

www.SimonSays.com

....

Keep up on the latest new
releases from your favorite
authors, as well as author
appearances, news, chats,
special offers and more.

SIMON & SCHUSTER
A VIACOM COMPANY
www.SimonSays.com

Pocket
Books